DUMB
AS
ME

Women Gave Him Pleasure, Misusing Them Gave
Him More

A
Michael Gainer
Novel

DUMB AS ME

Women Gave Him Pleasure,
Misusing Them Gave Him More

PLUTONIUM PUBLISHING, LLC
MIAMI, FLORIDA

Published by:
Plutonium Publishing, LLC
18520 NW 67th Street Suite 278
Miami, Florida 33015

Library of Congress Control Number: 2002107152

ISBN 0-9714887-0-3

Dedication

*This book is dedicated in loving memory
of my sister. My mother's daughter.
Pamela Zenora Moore-Johnson.
We miss you.*

Are you watching the
game, playing the game, or don't even
know the game exist? After reading Dumb
As Me, be sure to peak at the "Tips Of The
Pimpin' Trade" at the rear of the book.

This book is full of deception, betrayal, and sex. I wrote this book to give you a glimpse into the life of a man who was lost in his own selfish desires. It's lonely to have the world and have no control over yourself. This is the story of my life, Justin Drake. I challenge you to read this book in the hope that you don't make the same dumb ass mistakes I did. So, if you're ready, turn the page and enter my world.

Introduction

In all the things running through my mind, I couldn't think of one thing that could make the situation better, any lie would only make matters worse.

I thought I would just screw her a few times and dump her. I just didn't know the sex would be so good. She was everything I'd dreamt of. I'm losing sleep thinking of the love we made. Now I'm crossed up about to lose everything I love. Over what . . . a good piece of ass!

We were going out for three months before I knew her last name. It didn't matter, I never called her by that name anyway.

Now I'm butt naked, hiding in this small closet, looking through a crack in the door. I'm not going out like this.

Chapter One
The Stock Exchange

It all started one Sunday afternoon. It was a
beautiful day, one of the best days of the entire summer.
Not too hot, it was the perfect day to be at the beach.
There was a light breeze blowing. I could smell the soft
scent of salt in the air, it almost smelled like money.
I was just hanging out with my boys on the beach.
You know, drinking, talking shit, telling lies, and disre-
specting women. The usual immature stuff men do. I was
feeling good. Full of that Hennessy amongst other things.
Mind wondering, rock hard, and surrounded by all those
fine women. Then, all of a sudden, the baddest woman I
had ever seen mesmerized me. My gaze became clear, my
speech pattern changed. I knew then she would be the
next woman I would misuse. I was fantasizing, I could

just feel myself inside her. That warm, wet, deep,
tight . . .Who-weee, I had to have her. I laid back and
played it cool. That's what pimps do. I wanted to see if
she would choose me. She made her rounds. Damn, it
seemed as if she knew every person out there. That's cool
too. I thought slut action, she'd let all the boys hit it. Men
do that every now and then. Get an animal on the side that
all the boys can run up in. Action like that is scary, because it can kill you.

As she moved through the crowd it gave me time
to observe her. I had to have it, I mean her. This woman,
her skin was caramel, more like caramel swirl. She was
about five feet ten inches tall, her breast were at least a
38C. Her mid drift was exposed. Baby's stomach was
ripped! Legs long and thick, with a slight bow, and that
ass, she had ass for days. Not an average ass, she was a
goddess. I wanted to rush her, but that's what a buster
would do, so I laid back.

From a distance of about 20 yards our eyes met. I
paused looking directly at her. I wanted to see how long I
could hold her attention. At that moment, it was as if we
were the only people in the world. She walked, no, more
like glided towards me. Our eyes never lost contact. I
tapped my boy so he could witness this pimp shit unfold.
She was closing quickly, about five steps away. Slim

extended her hand as if she was about to introduce herself
when at that very moment, she tripped and stumbled
forward. It took everything in me not to laugh. My boys
thought that was the funniest thing they had ever witnessed. However, they remained composed as not to mess
up anything that was about to happen. I had to give her
credit, she gathered herself quickly. At that time we were
face to face, she introduced herself.
"Hello, my name is Embarrassed." She got jokes! I asked
her if she was okay. I was holding her hands looking
down at her, looking up at me. What a helluva way to
make an introduction. The one good thing that happened
was the ice was broken. I thought, please let that be a one
time slip on her part. Please Lord, don't let her be one of
those beautiful goofy chicks.

She told me her name was Eden. She explained
being with her was like paradise, like the *Garden of Eden*.
Yeah right, one man's paradise is another man's hell. She
went on talking about herself for five minutes. I pretended
to be very attentive and interested in what she was saying.
The entire time I was imagining her eating a popsicle. I
told her my name was Quincy, that wasn't my real name, I
just told her that. Hell, I'm a player, I have at least ten
different aliases. I was feeling like Quincy at the time.
How could she resist this venom I was about to spit.

As the night progressed our conversation became
more erotic. I was happy we made it to that point. It was
my time to shine. It was time for the sheep to be devoured
by the wolf. This was my comfort zone. I thought to
myself "once again, it's on." Before I could take control
of the conversation Eden asked, "can you fuck?" As my
Grandmother would say I was taken aback. She was using
my lines on me. I was supposed to ask her that. I was not
prepared to answer that question. Although I'd asked
hundreds of women that question and heard thousands of
responses, I didn't have one of my own. She saw the
hesitation on my part and took full advantage of the
moment, like a Pit Bull on a Chihuahua. She told me not
to answer just listen. My head was totally screwed up at
this point. She said, "I know you can fuck, but, can you
do it good?" We were standing at the time, I suggested we
sit and talk. I only made that suggestion because after the
question it made me hard. Not an average hard, hard
enough to cut diamonds, penitentiary hard. I finally
responded by saying, "I was good with mine."
"Good answer," she said. I felt like a real buster. That
was the only response I could remember. Some girl told
me that, so I used it. This was the first time in my journey
through a player's life-style I ever felt as though I needed
to check my game. Honey was on point, I knew I could

get into this woman, and that was scary.

Laughing and talking about dumb stuff, our conversation continued into the early morning hours. I was enjoying her company. I could tell she was feeling me too. Several times during the course of the evening, my boys told me some of my previous victims were inquiring as to why I was spending so much time with Eden. Stuff like, "is that his new bitch?" I saw a lot of scrubs looking at me out the corner of their eyes, they probably wish I was gay. One thing I can't stand is a player hater. Despite popular belief, all bitches ain't women.

I didn't mind spending time with a woman like Eden in public, because it raised the value of my stock. I knew my shit was about to go through the roof. One thing I've learned about women over the years, if they know someone has an interest in you, they want to find out why. Moreover, if the woman interested in you is fine, I mean fine like Eden, the other women must find out why she chose me. I guess it's in their nature.

We decided we enjoyed each other and wanted to spend more time together. We exchanged pager and cell numbers. That was an immediate red light. I didn't care, I just wanted to hit it. If she had baggage it didn't matter, she had to carry it. We both knew what time it was, so neither of us said anything. She told me to holla at her when I was free. I agreed I would call her, and before she could say a word, I turned and walked away. Always leave in control. I had to gain some control, because she had it all day.

"Quincy," she called out. I turned around slowly.

"What's up?"

"Do you have to go? Let me take you to breakfast. Would you like that?"

"Yeah that would be nice, do you have a spot in mind?"

"We can go to the diner on Washington."

"That's cool. I'll meet you there."

"No, let's walk. It's not far, come walk with me. Is that okay with you?"

"Yeah that's cool, lead the way." We walked down the street looking at each other. I definitely didn't know where this was going, but I had a damn good idea.

"Hold my hand Quincy," I gave her my hand. "Your hands are so big I feel so safe with you, put your arms around me." I put my arms around her flexing a little so she could feel how hard they were. She put her head up against my chest and rubbed her hand across my torso. She was just feeling me up to find out if I was in shape. My shit was tight, chest bulging and stomach rippling.

"Damn, Quincy you big!"

"I'm big all over."

"What, am I supposed to take your word for it?"

"You felt me, you know it's true."

"I haven't felt you yet." She reached down and grabbed my crotch. She moved her hand across me real slow, trying to determine how much of that bundle she was holding was dick and how much of it was balls. I decided I would make it simple for her.

"Take it out. That way you can see what your getting yourself into, or what's going to get into you."

"You're confident aren't you? I like that, I think it's sexy." We stopped in between two parked automobiles. "Be careful, you don't want to let this monkey out the bag." She unzipped my pants and pulled me out.

"Damn you're hard." She rubbed my penis against her chiseled body.

"Suck it baby, " I said.

"You want me to suck it? You want me to make you feel good?" She looked at me stroking me softly.

"Yeah, suck it." I said licking my lips.

"I ain't sucking nothing, put that thing back in your pants. The only way I'm sucking you is if you eat me first."

"That can be arranged."

"Quincy," she looked up at me as I zipped up my pants.

"Yes."

"Don't be so quick to give up the ass. It makes you look

cheap." This woman had game. We stepped out from
behind the van and made our way to the diner.

"Get us a table. I'm going to wash my hands."

"Yeah, you do that." Eden went to the rest room. I
watched her as she walked away. She was unreal. I
noticed several guys looking too, one even gave me the
thumbs up, expressing his approval. I grabbed a booth and
two menus. Eden returned from the rest room.

"Did you miss me? Move over I want to sit next to you."
Eden pushed me over to the wall. I felt like the girl. Her
aggressive nature turned me on.

"So did you wash that scent off your hands?" Eden
smelled her hands to make sure they didn't smell. We both
laughed.

"You're funny Quincy, I like you. You make me laugh.
They say if you can make a woman laugh you can sleep
with her. Do you think you can sleep with me Quincy?"
That was the second time she'd asked me a question like
that.

"I just know I can make you laugh."

"What are you going to order?" Eden asked, redirecting
the conversation.

"I need some grits, eggs and sausage. A real meal."

"I want the same thang." Eden called for the waiter.

"Garcon, Garcon."

"Girl you crazy," we ordered our food and had a nice erotic conversation. We laughed and joked until the sun came up.

"Quincy I'm getting tired. I have to go."

"That's cool, I understand." We walked out of the diner into the sunlit streets.

"Quincy, I'm going to catch a cab home."

"You don't have to do that, I'll take you."

"Are you trying to get in my panties Quincy?"

"Of course, but not today. You catch that taxi, call me."

"I'll call you soon baby." She flagged down a taxi. I kissed her on the cheek and walked away.

Chapter Two
Control

It had been six days since I'd spoken to or seen
Eden. I assumed she'd lost my number. She should have
called me. What was I saying? I don't sweat women, they
sweat me. Why was I concerned whether she called me or
not? Maybe I missed her page? I made it a habit of
turning off my pager when I went in the house. This was a
must do, I lived with the biggest player hater in the world,
my wife. Oh, you didn't know I was married? Yeah,
married with kids. That only made me more dangerous.

My wife knew I was an unfaithful man. We've
talked about it on several occasions, my infidelity. I didn't
think she suspected anything, because the house was
always taken care of. No matter how much of myself I
gave out in the streets, I still brought nine, rock hard
inches home. Besides, she was living lovely. Her job was

to look pretty, spend my money, and make love to me. I
knew at least one hundred women that would trade places
with her in a heart beat. Hell, she probably had a few men
on the side.

    It was Saturday, my wife always took the kids to
the mall and a movie. My time was short, I used this time
to talk to my freaks. So I thought, "let me make this call."
I went down stairs outside by the pool to use my cell
phone. I always used the cell to call women. A player
never calls from his house phone, women can be scandalous, oh so vicious. Caller ID and *69 have made many
players turn in their cards.

69 . . . ringing . . .

"Hello, may I speak to Eden?"

"Hi Quincy," she replied. I knew it, she'd been expecting
my call. I couldn't believe I called her first.

"How have you been? I've missed you." I said.

"I've missed seeing your handsome face, I'm wet from
just hearing your voice, I've masturbated twice this week
wishing you were inside me." She spoke in a sexy, allur-
ing voice.

"You don't have to use your fingers, you can use mine," I
said.

"I'd rather use your dick, can I use it?" What kind of

question was that, of course, did she think I was going to say no? I had to calm down and act as if this happened to me all the time.

"What would be a good time for you?" I asked.

"I'm wet right now, come to my condo, my address is 1000 Ocean Drive, Suite 3569."

I wanted to jump right on this, but it sounded like an okie doke.

"I'll be there," I told her. We both hung up. I thought this was perfect, another side was telling me that it couldn't be more wrong. She was the finest woman that I'd seen in life, and she was waiting for me. I had to get it.

• • • • • •

It was a beautiful day in the city. I decided to pull the convertible out. I never told you about me. What can I say, I was the shit. My real name is Justin Drake. I had everything a man could want. I guess I was living like a true baller. I had money, power, and women. The funny thing was I made it all honest. I made some sound investments, listened to the right people, then people gave me their money to flip for them. The investment business was the easiest thing in the world. I told you I was a pimp, a pimp never works for money. I earned a modest amount,

six figures a year. Being a pimp was a full time job, I
loved it.

I knew I was handsome. 6'5", 240 pounds of pure
Nigga. I worked out every day, if I were a woman I would
want me. I was a rich woman's dream and a poor
woman's fantasy. My home was nice. It was in an upscale
neighborhood in Miami. My neighbors were doctors,
lawyers, and professional athletes. Most of them were
pimps too, very few of them worked for money, they just
knew how to make it. I often thought about life, my life,
and laughed. I was just striving to maintain control in an
out of control world. My life was an illusion, Copperfield
could learn a lot from me.

Suite 3569 Penthouse, honey got loot. The majority of the women I met were broke, looking for a hand out
instead of a hand up. They soon learned if they came
messing with me, I'd break'em. Break their heart, mind,
body, and spirit. If they had a wallet, I'd break that too.

Eden left the key with the door man. A key was
required to access the penthouse. That was new for me, I
was feeling it. On the way up, I was in the elevator with
some real hillbilly types. They asked, "what floor?" Oh,
they didn't know . . . Penthouse Player! At least that's
what I wanted to say. I simply replied, "35 please."
Everyone exited the elevator before the thirty-fifth floor,

to go any higher you had to have a key.

"What's behind door number one?"

Chapter Three
What's Behind Door Number One?

The elevator doors opened slowly. It was almost as if I were in the Twilight Zone. I stepped out assured in a place I was not sure. Eden's place was unbelievable. The condo had an ocean view. The entire exterior was glass, everything was white, and the floors were marble, complemented with a walk around veranda. There was a huge salt water aquarium in the middle of the room, it was at least 1,000 gallons. The tank extended from the floor to the ceiling. All of the 14 sliding glass doors were open, which allowed a brisk breeze to blow through. The place was breathtaking and empty. The only thing in there was a grand piano and a super king size bed. I must admit the crib was fly.

"Quincy is that you?"

"Yeah."

"I'll be out in a minute, make yourself a drink, there's a
bottle on the balcony." Eden was in the bathroom.
Women! Never ready or on time. This was the time to
plunder through her stuff, but there was nothing to plunder
through.
"Quincy, there are chilled champagne glasses in the
freezer, pour us a drink."
"Okay." I paused looking in the refrigerator, "Eden, what
are you doing?"
"I'm preparing myself for you." Fresh and sweet, that's
how I like it. Besides, I'd get full of that rock hard, champagne made me a sexual Tyrannosaurus. I got the champagne glasses out of the freezer. I walked out of the
kitchen onto the balcony. I strolled half way around the
building before I found the bottle chilling in ice. It was
the only thing on the balcony. The view was incredible.
"Hi Quincy, sorry to keep you waiting." I turned slowly.
What I saw was unreal. She was more remarkable than I
remembered. She had on a full length chiffon dress with
nothing on underneath. The wind blowing against her
body revealed all of her assets. She had a very unusual
smell, it was almost intoxicating. Her hair was cut short
and styled nice, similar to Halle's. Her nails and toes were
manicured, she was perfect. I handed her a glass of
champagne. Finally I spoke.

"Hi, I've missed you."

"Tell me what you missed about me Quincy?" Damn, she had to ask that!

"I missed seeing your pretty face, the way you tilt your head when you laugh. I've missed you,

I've missed the thought of you." I waited for her to respond, but she said nothing, she just looked at me, as if she were looking into my soul.

"Come here." She walked towards the edge of the balcony. I poured myself another glass of champagne. I was afraid of heights and we were 35 stories up. The only thing keeping me from falling was a waist high rail. She grabbed my hand and pulled me towards her.

"Your heart is beating so fast," she said while rubbing her hand across my chest.

"You excite me." I was trying to conceal my fear.

"Do you want me?" I nodded my head slowly in an up and down motion.

"Take me," she said.

We began to kiss. I wanted to step inside of her body. My tongue seemed as if it couldn't go deep enough into her mouth. I grabbed her head very gently to control her movements. I did this so I could control myself. I was moving too fast. I slowed us down and she began to moan. I caressed her breast, while pinching her hard nipples. She became limp in my arms. I picked Eden up and carried her into the bedroom and laid her down on the bed, looking at her while I undressed. Eden looked at me as she sucked her fingers and inserted them inside of herself. I laid down on her, kissing and sucking her breast through her dress. I went down on her, licking and sucking, she was screaming my name.

"Quincy, Quincy, Quincy!"

I pulled her dress up slightly over her navel. I hesitated, looking into her eyes. She was lost in the love we were making. I put myself inside her. Eden screamed, wrapping her legs around me and squeezing. I stopped pumping so she would relax. I kissed and caressed her face slowly and softly. She opened her legs wide, like a rose in full bloom. I grabbed her legs and pushed them into the bed. I had her knees touching her elbows. She yelled, "GIVE IT TO ME! DO IT BABY! GET IT!" So I did for about 15 minutes. I was on a mission to please her. I flipped her over and hit it from the back. I slapped her on the ass and told her to "take this dick." Eden was leaning down reaching back squeezing my ass. She used her other hand to stimulate herself. Eden could sense I was about to unload. She began to squeeze and contract her vaginal muscles. I shot off like a roman candle. I fell to the side in ecstasy. She immediately started sucking me. I wanted her to stop, it felt so good it hurt. She was humming, licking my balls and all. My eyes rolled back in my head, my toes began to twitch.

"I'm about to explode!" I told her that because I didn't want to shoot off in her mouth. She didn't stop or slow down. I came so hard I thought she might choke. I never saw an ounce of semen.

She laid there with her head on my thigh, moving me around in her mouth. We looked at each other for about ten minutes before we said anything. It seemed like a lifetime. At that moment, I was content with a beautiful woman with smoking head. She began to suck me until I was hard again. She stood up straddling me. She pulled her dress over her head. She rubbed the dress across my face softly, teasing me. That was the first time I had seen her entirely naked.

"Do you like what you see?" I nodded yes. She bent down, slowly inserting me inside her. She was looking at me as if she could see through me, as if I belonged to her. Up and down, back and forth in a circular motion, she was riding me like a champ.

"Do you like me Quincy, do you like the way I feel?" Before I could answer she started to climax. As she was riding me, she leaned back slowly never breaking her rhythm. She quivered, grunted, and fell forward kissing me while she gazed into my eyes.

Chapter Four
A Gentleman Never Tells

A gentleman never tells. I told everyone I knew, all my boys. I couldn't hold this in, I struck gold and I had to tell it. I immediately called my boy Hammer. We called him Hammer because he nailed all the women.

"What up Hammer?"

"Ain't nothing, just chillin."

"You know I hit that right. That bad one from the beach."

"You hit it?"

"Yesss Playa, I beat it out!"

"Was it good?"

"I was good! Yo honey is a straight freak! She licks booty and all playboy."

"Damn son, you the man."

"Show you right, I'll holla."

"One!"

I remember Hammer lying telling me he screwed this girl twenty times in one night.

"Man, you know you're lying," I said while I looked at him out the corner of my eyes.

"Nah Money, I'm serious. I knocked her down twenty times in less than twenty four hours kid. We went through an entire tube of KY Jelly. I was like a machine."

"You're a machine all right, a lying machine."

Some stories were just too unbelievable to be real, that was one of the many I heard. We usually had these conversations anytime we had a new freak. I think we all lied to make our stories better. Only this time I was telling the truth. Eden was the bomb and she had my nose wide open.

Chapter Five
Rehabilitation

Page 23, Section A, line 17b of the Player's In-
structional Manual. Never have sex with the same woman
twice, one of the principles I didn't follow. Eden was like
crack. Her body was calling me. I needed to check
myself into rehabilitation. I didn't know Eden but I had an
uncontrollable desire to be with her. I needed to spend
some time with my wife.

"Honey."

"Yes Justin."

"Let's go to New Orleans."

"We can't go to New Orleans, at least not without the
kids."

"We can drop them off at my mothers, you know she loves
her grand babies. What do you think?"

"Lets go."

      Guilt had set in. I was usually ultra nice after I had messed up. My wife often stated I was the sweetest man she'd ever known. That gives you an idea of how much I screwed around. She would get mad and throw me out every now and then, but she always got over it. We'd make love and it's all good.

"When are we leaving?" She asked excitedly, anticipating the trip.

"We'll take the children to my mother on Thursday and catch a flight to New Orleans Friday evening."

"How long is your mother going to baby sit?"

"I don't know, long enough for us to have a good time, I guess about 10 days, what do you think?"

"That sounds good."

"Let me give her a call." I needed to come up with a good lie, she usually saw right through most of them. I decided to tell her the truth.

"Hello, may I speak to Sylvia?"

"This is Sylvia."

"What's up cuz, what they do?"

"Boy don't call my house with that foolishness."

"Yes Mama. I was wondering if you wanted to spend some time with your grandchildren this summer?"

"Sure, you know I can't get enough of those babies."

"Great, we'll be there on Thursday."

"Thursday, wait a minute!"

"I love you Ma, gotta run, bye!" I hung up the phone quickly. I hoped she didn't call me back. I took the phone off the hook just in case.

"It's on baby." Alexis was walking out of the room with her purse.

"Where are you going?"

"I'm going to the mall, I don't have anything to wear."

"Nothing to wear, you have three closets full of nothing to wear."

"Justin, you like me to look good don't you?"

"You know I do."

"Well, I'll be back soon. The kids are upstairs."

"Okay." I didn't believe she was going to the mall, all them damn clothes she had. "Be careful, I love you."

It's strange how people use the word love so freely. Love, I love you, love me. These are probably the most powerful, misused words in the English vocabulary. I was guilty. I used these words when I didn't mean them. "I love you" seemed to have some mysterious effect on women. Funny thing is that it has the same effect on men. I often questioned myself when I told my wife I loved her. The question was did I really mean what I said? I guess I felt guilty because I disrespected our wedding vows daily.

I needed this time with her. I figured this trip would give us a chance to talk and catch up. We lived in the same house but had two very separate lives. We needed this mini vacation. I needed it for us. But, before we left I had to call my freaks. Who's first on the list?

Chapter Six
Who's First On The List?

E-mail, voice mail, pagers, cell phones, and text messengers are all effective ways of communication. Technology allowed this player life-style to go to another level. I had my freaks on speed dial, listed under my different aliases.

19 . . . ringing . . .

"Hello."

"Hi baby, how are you?"

"Who is this?"

"You know who it is."

"Fred?"

"That's right the man that gets you off." It was a moment of silence, as if she was thinking about the last time we were together.

"You sure do. Where have you been? I haven't seen you lately."

"I've been working hard trying to earn a living, you know me."

"Yeah, I know you all right, you don't work."

"I can work this dick if you let me."

"When?"

"I'll call you back in about 45 minutes, bye." I hung up and called the next one on my list.

26 . . . ringing . . .

"Hi sexy."

"Tony, I've missed you, where have you been? I beeped you."

"You have . . . my pagers been messing up lately. So, whatcha you doing right now?"

"Nothing, wishing you were here."

"You want me? You want me there inside you?"

"Yes."

"Check this out, I want the same thing. Can I call you back in an hour?"

"Yes."

"Okay . . . later."

6 . . . ringing . . .

"Hello, may I speak to Erica?"

"Hold on . . . Mom, telephone."

"Hello."

"Where your man at?"

"I'm talking to him." That's just what I wanted to hear.

"Have you missed me?"

"I always miss you Chris, you my Boo."

"I love it when you say that, I need to see you."

"Well, I need to get a sitter." I thought yes you do, because I won't be able to get any with those bad ass kids running around.

"How long will that take?"

"Not long, I just need to call my sister."

"Okay then, I'll call you back."

"All right . . . in a minute."

11 . . . ringing . . .

"Hello, is Sandra in?"

"May I ask whose calling?"

"Yes, this is Mr. Williamson with Pinnacle Funding."

"Hold on. Sandra, telephone." Ten seconds elapsed before she answered the phone

"Hello."

"Hello Sandra, this is Mr. Williamson, did I catch you at a

bad time."

"No Mr. Williamson, this is not a bad time?"

"Damn, I hate it when your old player hating ass husband answers the phone . . . anyway, can you get out?"

"I'm not sure about that stock, I'll have to do some research."

"I need to see you."

"Can I reach you at your office?"

"Yeah, hit me when you get a minute."

"Okay, I'll look into that right away."

"Can I eat you?"

"I've always wanted to invest in that stock."

"Well come get it, call me . . . bye."

69 . . . ringing . . .

"Hello."

"Eden?"

"Hi, I thought you were done with me." *Done? Done? I was just getting started.*

"I've missed you. I enjoyed the love we made. Now how could I be finished with a woman like you?"

"Quincy we didn't make love, you beat it out."

"Can we do it again?"

"A fuck is out of the question. I'll make love to you next time."

"That's cool . . . so can I come over?"

"Wait . . . the elevator doors just opened, my other lover is here. Sorry, next time, miss me." Eden said in a whispering voice as she hung up the phone.

I knew she had a man. He was over there getting that sweet ass. Damn, I felt like she was cheating on me. I was tripping, well I had four other chicks lined up. I really wanted to see Eden. That's exactly why you set up more than one date at a time. Women run game too. They will tell you its on, but they have other intentions. I didn't get mad. That's the name of the game. If you're going to play it, then you must respect it. No doubt one of these chicks would come through, they always did, with legs and mouth open. Don't hate the player, or the game. I made my way back in the house, still thinking of Eden and another man.

"Justin?"

"Upstairs baby." My wife returned home from the mall, she came up to the kids room. The kids and I were chilling playing video games.

"Did you buy the mall?" I asked.

"Funny, you got jokes, no I just bought a few things for our trip."

"What did you get for me?"

"I bought you some lingerie."

"You know what I like, come show it to me." I stood up and left the kids playing their game. We went into our bedroom.

"Did you enjoy yourself baby?"

"Yes, you know I love to shop."

"Yeah I know, you've been gone about four hours. I was beginning to worry."

"Why didn't you call me?"

"I guess I just wanted to give you some time to enjoy yourself. Anyway, I'm glad you're home."

"You're so sweet, I'm safe here with you now. I have a surprise for you."

"You do?"

"Yes, but you'll have to wait until we get to New Orleans."

"That I can do . . . check this out, I'm going out for a while. I'll probably hang out with James, Rick, and Juan. I won't be long."

"Okay baby."

That gave her time to get herself together. I know she wasn't shopping all that time. Four hours at the mall and she only came back with one bag, what I look like?

Chapter Seven
Illusions

I had to knock off one of these chicks before I left. Damn, I couldn't stop thinking about Eden. I knew what would take my mind off her . . . PUSSY. I called my freaks to see what was up. I talked to all of them with extreme confidence. They knew what I was calling for . . . that ass.

19 . . . ringing . . .

"Hello."

"Yeah, what's up, can I see you?"

"I can't, something's come up."

"That's cool, I'll call you later."

"Okay baby, call me . . . bye."

Something came up . . . Yeah, another man beat

me over there. That's what came up. She was talking all
soft whispering on the phone. I knew the game . . . life
goes on, I just called the next one.

26 . . . ringing . . .

"Hello."

"It's me."

"Hey you, I thought you were going to call me earlier."

"I got caught up . . . so can I see you?"

"I'm going out with my friends." Damn! The trick was to
act as if it was no big deal.

"Where are you going?"

"I don't know, somewhere on the beach."

"Okay, enjoy yourself, I'll talk to you later, have a good
time."

I didn't want to come by anyway. The first time I
went to her house, I thought we were going to get down,
but she had other plans. She pulled out this 18 inch dildo,
laid down, and put the whole thing inside her, all 18
inches. She liked it in all her holes. I looked down at my
Johnson, I was about 9 inches short. I couldn't do anything with that, I just watched her freak herself. I grabbed
the dildo from her and slapped that ass a couple of times.
Although, she had good head, I needed some guts.

6 . . . ringing . . .

"Hello."

"Erica, the love of my life, what's up?"

"Nothing now, I've been waiting for you two hours."

"I'm on my way."

"Too late, I just picked up my kids."

"Damn, I'm sorry. I got caught up."

"I was going to put it on you to."

"You were, tell me about it baby," I said grabbing my crouch.

"I ain't telling you shit. I'm over here all wet and you can't do shit about it."

"I'm sorry. Let me come over, I just want to put the head in."

"No."

"I'll make it up to you."

"When?" She asked sarcastically.

"I'll call you . . . bye." I hung up the phone in disgust.

Damn, I was down to my last freak. Sandra, she probably had the best pussy out of all the women. Her husband was an older man. She told me he could eat it better than me, but he couldn't beat it better than me. I told myself if I ever met him, I'd tell him to put a pillow under that ass, she liked that.

11 . . . ringing . . .

"Hello Sandra, its Mr. Williamson."

"I know, I've been expecting you."

"Can you talk?" I asked anticipating a yes.

"Yes."

"Can you get away?"

"I'm going to the mall in about five minutes, I'll call you
when I get back."

"Okay, bye."

Sandra was my little married freak. She didn't get
out much, her old player-hating husband kept her locked
up, but when she did get out, she got loose. We talked in
codes, it was fun. She liked the excitement of it all.
Sandra believed the sex was good because it was scary
sex. I liked Sandra, she was down for what ever and
where ever. She liked it raw, I must admit it did feel good.
It was also stupidity on my part, I know I should have
checked myself.

"Ahh . . . Ah . . . Ahhh." I said to her as I grabbed her
shoulders and pressed my chin in the side of her neck.

"Cum in me." She moaned, holding me down on her so I
couldn't get up.

"Catch it baby . . . catch it." I wonder if her husband
knew he was sucking my dick when he ate her out?

"That was great baby. Do you have something in your

truck I can wipe my self with?"

"Yeah . . . there are some baby wipes in the glove compartment." I reached over Sandra to get the wipes out.

"You missed me a lot?" She said pressing the wipes against her vagina.

" Why do you say that?'

"You came so much . . . it's running out of me like water."

"Don't let it get on my seats!" I hurried and gave her the entire pack of wipes.

I think she liked going home with my scent on her. It added more risk to the game she liked to play. I often wondered what Sandra would do if we ever were caught? After she cleaned herself up she got out of the truck and headed home. I did the same.

69 . . . ringing . . .

"Hello."

"Hi darling."

" Quincy! Where have you been?"

"No where yet . . . I'm going to New Orleans on Thursday."

"Will I see you before you leave?"

"Of course."

"I want us to make love, I need you inside me."

"Are you busy?"

"No, are you coming over?"

"Go outside on your balcony, look down at the beach.

Look, do you see me, I'm waving . . . can you see me?"

"Yes I can see you, what are you doing?"

"Can I come up?"

"Yes." I rushed to Eden.

"Hey, bring that thing over here."

"You want me, do you want me?"

"Yes Quincy, I want you, I want you in me, on me, I want you."

Suddenly I felt a hard shove on my shoulder.

"Justin, Justin . . . wake up. Wake yo drunk ass up, wake up . . . what are you dreaming about?"

"I'm up, I'm up."

"What were you dreaming about?" Alexis shouted while shaking my shoulder.

"I was dreaming about you . . . I was dreaming, I was making love to you. What time is it?"

"You probably was dreaming about one of your ho's."

"No, I was dreaming about us."

"Yeah right, get up. It's time for you to get up, we're going to miss our flight. We need to be at the airport in one hour."

"I'm up, I'm up."

Chapter Eight
Almost Paradise

Hot-lanta. I'd forgotten how beautiful it was. I
had a lot of memories there, good and bad. I was looking
forward to seeing my mother, we had not seen each other
since the New Year. I'd been running my business and
running the streets, I hadn't made much time for her.
Besides, if it were not for her, Alexis and I would have
been divorced two children ago. Every time we decided to
split for good, Alexis became pregnant. I think she did
that based on advice from my mother. Two beautiful
children came out of the relationship. I often wondered
where I would be if we were not together.
"Look kids, there's your grandmother." The kids ran to
my mother screaming. They really loved her. I looked at
my wife as the children ran to my mother. Alexis gazed at

my mother as though she hated her, or, she hated the way the children felt about their grandmother. I think she resented my mother for convincing her not to divorce me and giving me children. Alexis caught me cheating more than once. She never said anything, but her actions spoke so loudly I often couldn't help but hear what she was saying.

I know why I cheated on my wife. There was only one logical conclusion, I was a coward. So I prepared myself for the day my wife couldn't take it anymore. When she left me, I believed all the affairs I had would make the stress of divorce less painful. In some strange way, it gave me some control in the relationship.
"Mom how are you, its so nice to see you." My wife added to the procession of greetings,
"Hi Ms. Sylvia, nice to see you."
"Nice to see you both, give an old lady a hug. Girl, you're getting so thin, you need some meat on those hips. Have you been taking care of my boy?"
"Yes, I've been taking care of your boy." I could sense the dry conversation going in the wrong direction. They just pretended to get along for my benefit. I knew they couldn't stand to be in the presence of one another. I had to whisper to my wife to chill out, we'd be in New Orleans tomorrow.

On the way from the airport we rode through the old neighborhood. I saw my first girl friend standing in front of her mother's house. "Damn, she'd gotten fat." I remembered sneaking in her window at night, every night as a matter of fact for six months. The only thing that stopped us was her monthly cycle, and sometimes that didn't matter. Now that I think about it, I've always been nasty. I was fifteen years old and doing dumb shit. I was going up in her bare back raw. We both had a total disregard for any type of birth control. After six months of straight raw sex the inevitable occurred.

"Damn girl you gaining weight, you need to do some push ups or something. Nah, you need to do some push aways, push away from the table."

"Justin, I think I'm pregnant."

"Pregnant, how you let yourself get pregnant? Well, it ain't mine!" I replied with a look of disbelief.

"What do you mean it ain't yours, I ain't been with nobody but you."

"Yeah right, ain't no telling who else you've been giving it up to. It ain't mine, it ain't mine."

That was the last time I ever talked to Lisa. I don't know what she did about the situation, all I remember was she stayed out of school for about a month. When she returned, she appeared to have lost the extra weight she was carrying the previous months. I've been mistreating women since I was a boy. I still behave like a child in many ways.

"Momma."

"Yes son."

"What did you cook?" I asked.

"Cook, I didn't cook anything. I didn't know you wanted me to."

"You know I love your cooking. It's been a while since I've had a home cooked meal."

"Your wife doesn't cook for you?" My mother said looking at Alexis.

"Oh yeah! My baby cooks for me and cooks well. Don't you baby?" Alexis looked at me rolling her eyes.

We arrived at my mother's house. The kids jumped out running to the swing on the front porch. My mother purchased a huge plantation style house a few years ago. It had a huge porch with a swing, breakfast table, and southern style rocking chairs. It looked like something out of a movie.

That evening we had a pleasant dinner. Bologna sandwiches and potato chips. My mother did that on purpose. She refused to cook. She wanted Alexis to cook something so she could critique it. Alexis was born at night, but not last night. She didn't fall for what she

deemed my mother's petty games. So we all enjoyed
those bologna sandwiches.

"So Mom, what's been up?"

"Nothing son, same thing different day. Henry has been
trying to get next to me. He asked about you and the
children. Why don't you take the kids to see him."

"For what, that's not their grandfather. He's not my
Daddy he just made me."

"Don't be like that, you have to let all that anger go, it's
going to destroy you."

"No it ain't, it keeps me going. Where was he when I
needed him? Where was he when *we* needed him. What
about when we didn't have money to pay the bills. We
were living in the dark while he was laid up with his
woman. He's a bum Mom, a bum!"

"Don't talk about your father that way, he is still your
father."

"I hear you but I don't want anything to do with him and
he'll have nothing to do with Logan or Lauren. Mom I'm
serious, don't take my kids over to see that man when I
leave. I'm serious, please."

"I'll respect that son. You're just like your father, so full
of fire."

"That's where you're wrong Mom, I'm nothing like him.
No matter what I do, I still take care of my family. Listen

baby girl can we drop this?"

"Sure Justin, sure son let's drop it."

"I love you Mommy. I'm going to bed. I'll see you in the morning." I kissed my mother and went upstairs to the bedroom. Alexis was in front of the mirror brushing her hair. She noticed the look of concern on my face.

"What's wrong baby?" Alexis asked walking towards me.

"Nothing, I don't want to talk about it."

"Is every thing okay?"

"I just had a conversation with my mom about Henry."

"Your father?"

"No, the dick I rode in on, Henry!"

"Why do you hate him so?"

"He was never there for us. We needed him. I needed him. I don't want to talk about this Alexis. I just want us to enjoy each other, can we do that?"

"Yes baby, we can do that." Alexis held me tightly. I fell asleep in her arms.

Chapter Nine
The Big Easy

New Orleans, the Big Easy, I planned to indulge my self in all its pleasures. Oh yeah, I forgot, I was here with my wife.

"Come here baby. I'm glad I'm here with you. I really wanted us to spend this time alone. Let's lock up in the hotel room and make love."

"That was my plan anyway. You seem to always know what I'm thinking. Sit down, relax, and order us some champagne and appetizers, I'm going to freshen up." Alexis went into the bathroom.

I'd forgotten how beautiful she was. Alexis had the total package, brains, body, and good pussy. The sex was incredible. Whenever I asked myself why didn't I leave her for another, her beauty and intellect quickly reminded me. However, I did realize her intellect would probably leave me in the poor house. Moreover, she was too fine to just let go. Eden was the only other woman that could hold a candle to her.

"What type of appetizers do you want?" I asked looking at the menu.

"The only thing I'm hungry for is you," she said from inside the bathroom.

"Well come out of the there, I've got something you can eat."

"Come in here," she said.

"You ain't said nothing slick to a can of oil!"

I went into the bathroom. My wife was in the roman tub, her naked body was partially exposed. She arched her back so I could see what was waiting for me. Her freshly shaved vagina pierced through the bubbles like the morning sun across the horizon. Her waist length hair was placed in eloquent disarray. I stood there in awe of her. Alexis was everything I wanted yet I misused her. We made love until the water became cold. I think that's the closest I'd ever felt to my wife. At that moment in time I only wanted her. After we made love she washed her body and mine. I had to relax and enjoy the moment. Alexis got out of the tub, dried her body, and dressed in front of me.

"Justin, I'm going downstairs to get some breakfast.
Come down when you get out of the tub."
"Okay, I'll be down in about 15 minutes." I let the water
out of the roman tub and stepped out. I heard three hard
knocks on the hotel door. I thought Alexis had forgotten
her key.
"Housekeeping."
"Wait a minute." I yelled trying to scramble for a towel.
Before I could say stop to keep the maid from coming in,
we were face to face staring at each other. It was the
longest ten seconds of my life. I think it seemed so long
because I was naked and beaded with water. The water
was trickling from the head of my penis. The house
keeper was trying not to look down, but she couldn't help
it. I didn't mind because I'm hung. I think I saw her lick
her lips. Look up! Damn, she couldn't stop looking at
me.
"I'll be out of your way in a few minutes." I reached for a
towel and wrapped it around my waist.
The housekeeper replied, "take your time, I'll come back
later." She turned to walk out the room, as she walked
out, she looked back at me. I quickly dressed and made
my way downstairs.

Brunch was great. My wife and I laughed and
joked about who climaxed the most. She boasted that she

had four orgasims all back to back. I often wish that I had
that capability. I guess there is a reason men can't have
multiple orgasms. If I came four times back to back I
would probably pass out. I didn't tell my wife what
happened with the house keeper. I didn't think it was a
good time to discuss another woman seeing my naked
body. Besides, I was in rehab.

Alexis asked, "are you ready?"

"I'm always ready for you baby."

"Not sex you silly goose, are you ready to take me shopping."

"Oh yeah, sure, I'm ready, lets ride."

  The French Quarter, French Market, and Magazine
Street, shopping, it was an all day thing. I rarely went
shopping with my wife. I found it difficult to window
shop. Why do women window shop? I know what I want,
I go to that store, buy it, and go home. It was a must for
Alexis to go in every store.

"Come Justin, let's go into this boutique." I followed
reluctantly, but I didn't have much say so in the matter, I
was being led by the hand. "Look at all the beautiful
things they have. Sit down over there, I'll just be a few
minutes." Alexis was running through the boutique like a
chicken without a head, picking up everything in her view.

"Justin, do you like this dress?" She asked holding the

dress against her body looking in the mirror.

"Yes I like it. It will look very nice on you."

"I'm going to try it on, come with me." I think I could have gave Job a run for his money. Although, I must admit I loved to sit in the dressing room and watch her undress.

"How does this look, do you like it? Does it make me look fat?" She said looking at her profile in the mirror.

"No baby, you look nice."

"Okay, I want to buy this." She took off her dress. Alexis was standing there naked, so I begin to lick her stomach.

"Stop, stop," she whimpered. "Lower, lower, lick lower baby." I was kissing her perfect body. I went down to taste her juices. I couldn't get to her like I wanted to due to the confined space. I was sitting and she was standing. I told her to put one of her legs up on the bench. I placed my hands under her ass and pushed her up as she rest her back against the wall, spreading her lips allowing me to taste her. It felt like I was drawing the vital essence of what made her a women out her body. She was grinding and gyrating her hips, grabbing my head and moaning very softly. I asked her did she want me, she told me to stop, then pushed me back and pulled me out and begin to suck it like a champ. I was trying not to make too much noise because the dressing room was packed. Her head was so good I wanted to scream. Alexis stopped sucking, she asked me to stand up. She turned around with her back facing me, bending over holding me in her hand. Alexis put me inside her silky wet body.

We were looking at each other in the mirror while she covered her mouth to muffle the sounds of ecstacy she was experiencing. "Not in me, okay." She said softly, not wanting me to release myself in her because she didn't have anything to wipe herself with. I came in her anyway. We wiped our selves on that pretty dress I liked. We took a few minutes to collect ourselves before leaving the dressing room. Alexis put the stained dress back on the rack and purchased another. I know it was nasty, but what else were we supposed to do?

Alexis put on her beautiful dress that night. We decided to go dancing.

"Come on dance with me, this is my jam." Alexis pulled me out on the dance floor. She turned facing me holding my hands. I was in cool mode so I just rocked from side to side clapping every other beat.

"Go baby it's your birthday, go baby it's your birthday." Alexis put on a show. She broke it down putting her hands on her knees and went old school. She was scrubbing the ground. I got right behind her grabbing her by the waist slapping that ass as she shook it one cheek at a time.

We danced the night away.

"Boy you know you crazy," Alexis said as we walked of the dance floor. "I didn't know you could still move like that."

"You're not half bad yourself. You messed my head up when you did the Do-Do Brown."

"Liked that huh?"

"Yessssssss!"

"Be a good boy and I'll do it again when we get back to the room." Alexis was glowing. I could tell she enjoyed herself. This was how we should have been all the time.

● ● ● ● ● ●

Two days later, same stuff different day. I was enjoying Alexis. She was truly my soul mate. I constantly told my self that so I'd believe it. Although, I was still yearning for Eden, I couldn't get her out of my head. Alexis asked me to get some ice, I agreed and told her I would be right back. I walked down the hall towards the ice machine.

"Hello Mr., how are you?"

"Fine thank you."

"Are you enjoying your stay in New Orleans?"

"Yes thank you." It was the house keeper that enjoyed the

peep show. I made idle chatter with her.

"Nice to see you again," I said.

"Not as nice as the last time I saw you," she replied.

"When can I see you again?" I was shocked, not surprised this chick was flirting with me. I decided to entertain her.

"When do you want to see me?"

"Right now," she replied with her hands on her hip standing wide legged.

It was perfect, she had the pass key to all the rooms in the hotel. We could go in any room right now. So, I decided to take her up on her offer.

"Lead the way," I said.

I looked at the housekeeper as she walked down the hall. Her ass was real plump and high on her back. She was no beauty queen, but she was fine as a five dollar pork chop, real thin with nice breast. I was thinking this was going to be a fun quickie. I'll just pull her skirt up, bend her over, and hit it doggie style. What was I doing? My wife was three doors down. This was too crazy, I couldn't do it.

"Look slim, I appreciate the offer and you are very attractive but I can't do this."

"What?" She said.

"I can't do this."

"What are you, gay?"

"Gay . . . Gay? I've been a lot of things but never gay."
That's what all women say when you don't want to be
with them, "he must be gay." I started to curse her out. I
just told her, "maybe next life time." I turned and walked
away. I was just going to get the ice and go back to my
room. As I was getting the ice out of the machine, I saw
this image out the corner of my eye. I turned my head
very slowly, it was the house keeper. She was just standing there not saying anything, just standing there looking
bizarre.

"May I help you?" I asked.

"No, you can't help me. Maybe that woman you're with
can help me . . . ask her if she wants to fuck." I thought, I
know she didn't just try me like a duck?

"What's your problem lady?"

"All you uppity Niggas think ya'll the shit . . . you ain't
shit. I'm throwing this pussy at you and you don't want it,
you must be gay!" This chick was crazy. She didn't know
me, I'm crazy too.

"You want this? Do you want this dick? Let's do it
then!"

I left the ice bucket right there, grabbed the maid
by her ass, and walked down the hallway. I thought she
would be an unwilling participant after I clowned on her,
it was as if she was more willing. This freak liked it. We

went into one of the rooms she was supposed to clean. I
turned to put the safety lock on the door. When I looked
back, she was stepping out of her uniform.
"So, you really want this huh?" She didn't say anything.
She just looked at me pulling down her panties and un-
strapping her bra. I only had on a t-shirt and shorts, I was
out of that in ten seconds flat. I looked at her holding
myself in my hand, thinking she didn't know who she was
fucking with. I made a decision to dig her back out.
"What are you going to do with that?" She asked. I
walked towards her very quickly. She reached up as if she
was expecting me to kiss her, I wasn't kissing her. I
grabbed her and we both fell to the floor. I was not going
to give her the satisfaction of screwing her on the bed. No
foreplay, no kissing, nothing. I shoved myself in her,
grabbing her legs and pushing them up. I then laid down
on her grabbing her shoulders, I was going to fuck her.
That's what she wanted, so I was going to give it to her.
"You like that, you like that huh ho? Do you like this?" I
said while thrusting myself in her. I was going as fast and
as hard as I could. I wasn't concerned about what she was
feeling or saying. I was on a mission to knock the bottom
out of that thang.
"I can't breathe." She muttered.
"Shut up bitch, take this dick."

"I . . . can't . . . breathe . . . you're . . . hurting . . . me." I
could feel myself throbbing, about to release. I raised up
on her looking down at her pain plagued face. I thrust
myself in and out of her as she tried to push me off. I
grabbed her head and pulled it close to my body, I wanted
to shoot all over her face.

"Catch it . . . Catch it ho." I said soft and stern. To my
surprise she opened her mouth and tilted her head back. I
looked down at my semen spewed all over her face. I
made sure that the majority of it went into her mouth.

"You like that? That's what you wanted?" I stood up
over her. At that moment I realized I was not in a hotel
with one of my freaks. My wife was down the hall. I
jumped in the shower to wash the smell of sex off me.

"Can I get in with you?" The housekeeper asked walking
into the bathroom. "No one has ever did it to me like that,
you got my legs shaking," she said standing in front of the
shower.

"Hell no, I'll be out in a second!" The shower curtain
flew open. "What do you want? I gave you some dick."

"You didn't give me nothing I gave you some pussy!"
She replied. "I just want to watch you bathe."

I cleaned myself up as fast as possible. I was careful only
to put the soap on my genitals. I couldn't go back to the
room smelling fresh out the shower. I dried my self off

and put my clothes back on.

"Thanks for the fuck," she said. I didn't say anything. I just hurried back to the ice machine to retrieve the bucket. Before entering the room I paused to catch my breath.

"What took you so long?" Alexis asked.

"I got into a conversation with the maid. Apparently some kids pissed in the ice machine on this floor. I went down-stairs to get some."

"How do you know they didn't piss in all the machines?" She knew I was lying, but what else was new.

"Never mind Justin, never mind. Lay down with me." I hoped she just wanted to cuddle, I didn't think I had another one left in me, at least not right then.

"Lay with me." I laid down with my wife, scared as hell.

"Your heart is beating so fast." Alexis was laying on top of me with her head on my chest.

"I took the stairs instead of the elevator, I needed to get a work out in."

"I'll give you a work out." Alexis rolled me over on top of her and we began to kiss. I asked her to hold me. Women love it when men talk like that, it makes us seem more sensitive. I wonder if when she told me to just hold her if she's just coming from having sex?

• • • • • •

Over the next couple of days I tried to avoid Sheila the house keeper. I thought she would have claimed I raped her. To my surprise, she act as if nothing ever happened. That was the best possible scenario.

New Orleans was a very enjoyable time for me and Alexis. Time spent away from the children, and other distractions always seemed to bring us closer. If I could only shake my desire to be with other women, our relationship would have been perfect.

"Justin, I miss my children."

"I miss them too."

"You know they are going to be really spoiled when we pick them up. They really love your mother."

"Yeah they do. We'll leave in a couple of days." I said.

"We'll be with them soon enough, 48 hours is not a long time. Besides, I've called them everyday. I just miss them that's all." Alexis said looking at a photo of the children.

"I know baby, I miss them too."

"Justin, let's go to the bar."

"Okay baby, whenever you're ready."

Alexis always had a drink or cleaned the house when she was depressed. If we were home the entire house would be spotless. That was a sure sign that something was bothering her. Since we're not home, her only

other option was to drink. I never said anything, I just
played along. It only took two drinks to turn that soft
spoken women into a flaming shit talker.

"Come on, let's go down to the bar." I hugged my wife
and told her we would leave tomorrow.

"Thanks Justin, I love you. I've really enjoyed our trip,
you're so nice to me. I just miss the kids."

"Shhh . . . I understand, let's go get that drink."

Chapter Ten
The Rooster

The next day we checked out and returned to
Atlanta to pick up the children. Alexis really missed
them. I was anxious to return too. I had some unfinished
business to take care of.

"Call your mother and let her know we're coming back
early."

"We'll just show up and surprise everyone, they won't
expect us this early. I know the children are probably
getting on her nerves by now."

"I doubt that, she'll put them back in line quick! They
know better."

"You're right, I'm going to check out, I'll meet you
downstairs. I'll send someone up for the luggage."

"Okay baby, I'll meet you in the lobby." I walked out of

the room on my way to the elevator. The elevator doors
opened and there stood Sheila the house keeper.
"Going down?" She asked. I stepped in the elevator. I
just gave her a hard stare, I was in no mood to entertain
her.
"You're leaving so soon? I thought I could get some
before you left." She moved close to me and ran her
ebony hands across my lips and then the side of my face.
"Are you going to miss me?" She asked. I grabbed her
hand and removed it from my face.
I answered dryly, "I'm going to miss everything about you.
Think about me." The elevator doors opened before she
could respond, we both stepped out at the same time and I
walked to the counter without looking her way.
"May I help you sir?"
"Yes, I'm checking out of room 1155."
"Is everything okay, we have you scheduled to check out
in two days."
"Yes, everything was fine, however, I'm checking out
today. Please send someone to the room to retrieve the
luggage, we'll be at the concierge waiting for the limou-
sine service to the airport."
"Right away Mr. Drake." I settled up with the hotel, I was
sure to leave Sheila the housekeeper a sizeable tip, maybe
she'd continue to keep her mouth shut. I decided to have a

drink while I waited for Alexis to come down. The bartender came over.

"What will you have?"

"Vodka." I said. I rotated the bar stool so I could see Alexis when she exited the elevator.

"Here you are sir, vodka, that'll be ten dollars." I gave the bartender a twenty and walked toward Alexis who seemed to be having trouble adjusting her slip dress.

"Is everything okay?" I asked.

"Yeah everything is good, the bellhop took care of everything."

"Great, do you want a drink before we leave?"

"No, just give me a sip of yours." Alexis took the glass from me and turned up my drink.

"Damn girl, you got a deep throat."

"I know, that's why you married me."

"True, are you ready baby?"

"Yeah, let's go." I signaled to the bellhop that we were ready. He loaded the luggage in the limo. I went to tip the bell hop when he informed me Mrs. Drake had already taken care of him. Sounded like one of my lines, but I had no time to dwell on that, my mind was on other pressing issues.

"So, did you enjoy your stay?" I asked Alexis.

"I loved it baby. You know I did, this was just the brief

vacation we needed."

"I enjoyed you too love." I leaned over and kissed Alexis on her peach colored lips. We arrived at the airport and took the next flight out.

• • • • • •

"I really think you should phone ahead to let your mother know we're here."

"No, I want to surprise the kids." I hailed a taxi.

"2002 Stone Mountain Road," I said to the taxi driver.

"Yes sir, right away." The taxi driver got out of the car and put the bags in the trunk. I opened the back door for my wife and we were on our way to Mom's house.

"I wonder what the children are up to?" Alexis asked.

"Just being kids probably. I hope they like the gifts."

"You know they will, video games, they'll love it."

We arrived at my mothers house about 30 minutes later.

"$46.35," the cab driver said.

"Damn, you sure that's right?" We exited the taxi, the driver opened the trunk and placed our luggage on the curb. "Here you are." I gave the taxi driver $46.35, since the trip was actually about $35.00. "He's trying to come up," I thought to myself. "Thanks," said the driver as he hit the curb when driving off.

"Alexis, go up to the house and ask the kids to come grab some of the luggage."

"Okay baby." Alexis walked up to the house and rang the bell.

"Do you think anybody's home?" Alexis asked trying to look through the windows.

"Yeah, they should be here."

As we were exchanging words, my mother came to the door.

"Hey," she said with a very surprised look on her face. "I didn't expect you all to return so soon."

"Hey Momma." I yelled from the street. "Tell Logan and Lauren to come out here."

"Are the kids in the back yard?" Alexis asked. "Kids, Momma's back! Where are you guys? Are you all hiding? Come give me a hug, I've missed you." Alexis was yelling at this point while walking through the house. By this time I'd managed to drag all the luggage into the house. Maybe I should have tipped the driver, my Louie luggage was taking a beating.

"Hey Momma." I bent down and gave her a kiss on her cheek. "What's wrong?" I asked. She had a troubled look on her face. "Mommy what's wrong? Is there something wrong with the kids?" She didn't answer. She just held her head down looking at the floor.

"Logan, Lauren get out here right now!" I yelled holding
my mother's hand.

"Honey, I can't find the kids anywhere. Ms. Sylvia, where
are *my* kids?" Alexis inquired sounding very concerned.

"Mom, are the kids okay?" I said in a very calm voice.
Alexis was beginning to panic. Her hands were covering
her mouth as tears began to flow.

"Mom, Mom, where are the children?" There was a
moment of silence, then she seemed to abruptly break out
of her momentary coma. Alexis was staring intently at me
as we awaited my mother's response.

"Son."

"Yes Momma."

"I took the kids . . ." She paused, and began to cry.

"It's okay Momma, tell us. You took the kids where?"

"I took the kids to spend the day with your father. I didn't
think you would be back so soon." I was relieved the kids
were okay. The way my Mom behaved lead me to think
the worse. Alexis also released a sigh of relief. She
walked over and leaned against my body. The relief I felt
was quickly replaced by anger.

"My children are where?"

"I took them to spend the day with your father." I looked
at my mother in disgust. Alexis was still leaning against
me. She quickly wrapped her arms around me and

squeezed me gently.

Alexis said in a soft tone, "Justin, Justin look at me. Calm down baby."

"Let me go!"

"No baby, calm down."

"Alexis— let me go!"

"Mom give me the keys to your car."

"What are you going to do?" My mother asked.

"I'm going to get my children. I asked you not to take them over there. I begged you and you did it anyway. Those are my children. Where are your keys!"

"Justin, I'm coming with you. I don't want you to do anything foolish." My mother finally went into her pocket and pulled out the keys.

"Foolish? The only one that has done something foolish is you." My mother drew back her hand and slapped me across the face.

"Don't talk to me that way!"

"I see things are still the same. You're still defending Henry. Don't take it out on me." I looked at Alexis, "get yo shit, we're leaving, call a taxi." I threw the keys to my mother's car on the kitchen counter. I went upstairs to the room where the kids' luggage was. My mother was right on my heels.

"What are you doing?" My mother asked. "I'm getting

my kids' things so once I get them from Henry we're
going straight to the airport."
"Don't do this Son, don't leave like this."
"Don't do it like what Mom? You did it Ma, not me . . .
you."
"Don't leave like this Justin. I'll take you Son. I'm sorry,
I'm sorry. I just want things to be right for everyone. I
just want things to be right." My mother was crying
holding both of my hands, shaking her head. I was mad,
mad as hell, but I couldn't stand to see her hurt. Hurt over
something that Henry had a hand in. It was my childhood
all over again.
"It's okay Mommy, take me to get the children."
"Okay son, okay."
My mother walked out of the room wiping her face.
"I'm going to the rest room to get myself cleaned up. I'll
be ready in a few minutes."
"Okay Momma."
"Alexis, come here." She walked into the room.
"Yes Justin."
"Help me get all of the kid's toys together, we're leaving."
"Justin don't leave your mother like this."
"What am I supposed to do Alexis, huh? Tell me, because
I could really use some help here."
"I don't know baby. I know you're hurt, but consider your

mother."

"I hear you baby, I hear you." I stopped and hugged Alexis. She was right. I did not want my personal feelings for Henry to ruin the relationship I had with my mother.

"I'll finish getting the kid's things and you go talk to your mother."

"Okay." I looked at Alexis and smiled. She was always more rational than me. I walked to the bathroom and knocked on the door.

"Mom are you okay?"

"Yes I'll be out in a minute."

"I just want to let you know that I love you and everything is okay. If I said anything that hurt you I'm sorry. Please forgive me." The door opened slowly. My mother emerged with blood shot eyes from the tears.

"There's nothing to forgive son. Are you ready?"

"Yes, we're ready." I returned to the room to find Alexis biting her nails.

"What's wrong?"

"I just want to go home. Me, you, and our babies. I just want to go home."

"Okay baby, as soon as we pick up the kids."

"Justin, promise me that you'll control yourself when you see your father."

"I hear you baby."

"I know you hear me, promise me."

"Let's go, Mom's waiting."

The ride over to Henry's was very quiet. You could feel the tension in the air. No one said a word. We pulled up to the house I grew up in. It was a shame to see how he'd let the place go.

"Mom look at this place. How . . .?" Alexis quickly cut me off to avoid another scene between me and my mom. I got out of the car, slammed the door, and went to the front of the house. I paused for a second to calm myself and pray. I looked back at Alexis. I motioned for her to come with me. I felt this shit was about to get ugly. Alexis stepped out of the car. I stepped up on the porch and knocked on the door.

"Who is it?" A man's voice sounded in reply.

"Justin Drake!" I could hear the kids screaming from the excitement of hearing my voice. The door opened and the kids flew out and wrapped themselves around my legs.

"Daddy, Daddy what did you bring us?"

"In a minute, say hello to your mother." I gestured in the direction of Alexis.

"Mommy, Mommy!" The kids ran to Alexis. I watched the kids and Alexis embrace and kiss one another. It was nice to see them safe. My feelings of love for my family

were interrupted by what seemed to be the voice of the
devil.

"Hello Son."

"Son? So I'm your son now?" I turned slowly facing the
man who called himself my father.

"Grow up Justin."

"Grow up, I'm as grown as you. Grow up? I've been
grown a long time. Grow up? Nigga catch up!"

"What you call me?"

"What did you hear? If you heard it I said it!"

"I won't allow you to disrespect me, I'm still your father."

"Father? Respect? You was just the rooster man. You
ain't never been a father. Now you over here playing
Grandpa. Nigga please."

"Get out of my house!" Henry pointed at the door.

"Your house, man this ain't your house, this my Momma's
house. Fuck this house." Henry clutched his teeth and
balled up his fist.

"Whatcha gone do? You better unball your fist and fix yo
face old man. I'm not that little boy you used to beat on."

"Get out of my house!"

"Yeah, whatever Henry, nice to see you again Daddy." I
backed out of the house leaving the door open. I walked
to the car and got in. Alexis had already ushered the
children into the car. My mother never bothered to get

out. We drove off slowly.

"Daddy, Daddy Grandpa brought us some toys. Can we
go back and get them?"

"Let grandpa keep them baby so he'll always have something to remember you by."

We went straight to the airport to catch a flight. I
assured my mother that everything was fine between us
and that I loved her. We embraced and I went into the
terminal.

Chapter Eleven
Reality Bites

It was nice to be back at my own house. It was time to put Justin on the shelf. I called my friend Hammer to find out what's up.

"Hammer!"

"What's up boy?"

"Just chillin, fresh off a road trip."

"You enjoyed yourself?"

"Yeah son, I had a marvelous time, you know kicking it with the wife . . . so what's up?"

"Still pimpin these slow ass ho's."

"True . . . so what's up for tonight? You gett'in out?"

"Yeah, I'm going to the club with Steve and James, you wanna roll?

"Fo sho!"

"All right, I'll hit you around 11:30."

"In a minute." I had to call my boys to let them know I was back. I had to go out, I needed to let my women know I'm back too.

"Alexis . . . Alexis . . ."

"Yes Justin."

"I'm going out with the boys tonight."

"Tonight, we just got here! You need to spend some time with your children, they miss their Daddy." She said pointing in the direction of the children.

"I know, I miss them too. I won't be out all night."

"That's what your mouth say, this is an all night thing."

"I'll stay home." I said sarcastically. Alexis told the children to go to their rooms.

"No, haul ass. I don't want you here if you don't want to be here. Haul ass . . . have a good time," she said opening the front door.

"Why are you talking to me like that?"

"You think you can just take me away, fuck me good for a week, bring me back, drop me off, and everything is okay? Well it's not okay. I'm tired of your shit. Just go, haul ass, have a good time."

"Why you tripping?"

"Why you going out? You going to meet yo bitch? Don't look away, answer me."

"What you talking about? I'm just going out, I haven't seen my boys in a week. I'm just going to hang out, that's all."

"What do I look like Justin? I know you believe I'm your fool. I'm not as crazy as you think. I see you."

"You see what? What do you see Alexis, huh?"

"I see you."

"Whatever." I went upstairs to the bedroom going directly to the closet to pick out something fly. I was going through all of my first string gear. I picked out the perfect outfit. I turned and Alexis was standing there blocking the entrance to the closet.

"What are you doing?" I asked.

"You ain't going no where motherfucker. I'm going to make sure of that."

"Girl look out! You better stop tripping."

Alexis had her hands behind her back. She swung her hands to the front of her body to reveal what she was hiding.

"What are you going to do with that?" She was holding a gallon of bleach. "Alexis I wish you would— You throw that bleach on my clothes. I swear to God I'll . . ."

"You'll what, you'll what Justin? What? Beat me, well beat me then!" Alexis drew back and threw the bleach in the direction of my clothes. I moved out of the way so she

could really get to it. She was yelling having a temper
tantrum.

"You ain't going no where." She pulled all of my clothes
out of the closet making one giant pile.

She looked at me standing over my clothes like a
prize fighter standing over a knock out. She tilted the
bleach and began to pour.

"How you like that? How you like that, Nigga!"

"You think you hurt me? That don't change shit. I'm still
going out. Look at you, you pitiful, just pitiful." I walked
away from Alexis, leaving her in the closet looking dumb.
I was mad as hell about my clothes, but I needed a new
wardrobe anyway. I never allowed Alexis to know that
she could hurt me. I went into the bathroom and turned on
the shower. I peaked back to see if Alexis was still in the
room. I could hear her rumbling.

"You better get your ass in here and clean up this mess." I
got in the shower, constantly peaking out. I was expecting
hot grits to come flying any minute. I stepped out of the
shower drying my self off rapidly.

"Alexis, where the hell are you?" She didn't answer. I
figured she'd taken the kids and left. That's her usual
mode of operation. I got dressed, put on some smell good
and was ready to roll. I was only able to salvage the one
outfit I had in my hand. It was the only thing not covered

in bleach. I looked back at my pile of multicolored clothes
and just shook my head. I paused for a brief second to
look at myself in the mirror. "Take that bitches!" Damn I
looked good.

Down the stairs and through the kitchen. I walked
in the garage, startled by the sudden emergence of bright
lights. Alexis and the kids were in her car. She opened
the garage door and backed out slowly.

"What are you doing? What's wrong with you?" I asked
walking towards the car shielding my eyes from the bright
lights.

"Fuck you Justin!" She hit the gas on the 6 and sped out
of the drive way. I was glad she was finally gone. She
was going to make me whip that ass. I wonder what Eden
was doing?

69 . . . ringing . . .

"Hello you've reached Eden, I'm not available please
leave a detailed message after the beep,
Beeeeeeeeeeeeeep."

"Hey gorgeous this is Quincy. I was wondering if you
wanted to hang out, I'm going to the club. Stop by if you
have time, if not I'll call you later. I miss you." I hung up
the cell and walked up the drive way. My eyes wide not
believing what I was seeing. "I know this— " Alexis had
flattened all the tires on the truck and one on the car. I

guess she stopped when she heard me come into the garage. That didn't change anything. I just had to change the tire. I couldn't believe she tried me like that, I couldn't believe it. I called Hammer to let him know I was going to be late.

    I constantly struggled, struggled with myself. I felt drunk or high at times, as if I were watching myself from a distance. The things I did, I knew were wrong. I may have a split personality, two different people. Beast versus gentleman. I was more comfortable being the beast, but I felt I was not in control. I didn't think I was willing to pay the price of losing my family. I didn't know if I cared. I cared, but not about myself. I felt as if I was crying out for help. Where does a man that has everything go when he needs help? I went where I was comfortable. Women gave me comfort, misusing them gave me more. I was feeling tired and sleepy because my thoughts reminded me of a fairy tale.

•   •   •   •   •

    Looking for love in the club. That's a no-no. In the club you're either looking for a freak or looking to be freaked. *"I just go to the club to listen to the music."* I hate to hear that line. It was no secret what I was looking for . . . that PUSSY.

"Justin, what's up son?"

"Just living large and taking charge . . . where them nasty sluts at?"

"They in here."

"All right Money, in a minute."

That was my man at the door. He was one of the bouncers here at the club. It was always a good idea to know who was running things. I was VIP, so I bucked the line and went straight to the front. It was also prime time. All those broke, fine ass women were looking, trying to figure out who I was. That's just all part of this pimp magic called the *Game*. You're either watching the game, playing the game, or being played. I found that most of the women I met were slow, slow to pick up on this pimpin game. By the time they figured it out, they were on their knees with my nuts slapping their chin.

"Yo, lets go upstairs." Hammer said pointing at the VIP section.

"Hold on Hammer, it's ho's down here." Never leave an area without making sure everyone in there has seen you. I tried to make brief eye contact with every woman I saw. It was like foreplay. They loved it.

"Yo, is that your lady?" Hammer asked.

"Which one . . . where?"

"Over there." Hammer pointed at a crowd of women. It was on! My little slice of paradise, Eden. I struck out from Hammer, giving him a pound telling him I'd holla at him later. I made my way over to where she was, brushing off the women that were grabbing my shirt and pulling on me trying to win my attention. Eden was standing in a circle of women having a conversation. I recognized some of them, they where known dykes. I stood outside of the huddle looking at Eden. When she looked up, she saw me and immediately excused herself from her entourage. We were standing in the middle of the club looking at each other. I knew that I was on stage, this was a live performance. My plan was to turn the place out.

"Hi love," I said.

"Love , that's a four letter word," Eden replied. She looked me up and down, rolling her tongue across her teeth as she rubbed my chest.

"Kiss me Quincy."

As I bent down Eden grabbed the back of my head and pulled me towards her, her mouth was slightly open. Both of our eyes were focused, we were looking at each other. Engrossed in our affection, I began to caress her breast and ass. I was still looking at her. Eden's eyes began to close slowly, she was really feeling me. Suddenly she unzipped my slacks, put her hand inside my boxers and began to squeeze my Johnson. I stopped kissing her, and just watched, she looked at me and continued to rub me. I tried to control myself, I didn't want to walk around the club with a hard on. Eden stopped and zipped up my pants.

"You don't want me Quincy?"

"Of course I want you . . . I always want you."

"I can't tell . . . you're not hard."

"We're in the club baby, you want it hard?"

"Yes."

"Tell your friends you're leaving." I pointed in the direction of the women she was standing with when Hammer spotted her.

"I'm here alone," she replied looking at what seemed to be her entourage. We walked out of the club hand in hand, amidst the gawking eyes of all the haters.

"Quincy, follow me."

"Where are we going?"

"Just follow me." The valet brought our cars around to the front of the club. Damn, I liked that chick, we hadn't seen each other for at least a month and we hadn't lost a beat. "Hold up!" I said. She had the same car as my wife. A Benz, 600 Series . . . sitting on 22's. I still didn't know what this chick did. I picked up my cell phone to call her to see what was up.

69 . . . ringing . . .

"Yes Quincy." Eden was looking at me through her rear view mirror.

"Where are we going?"

"Relax, it's a surprise. Just be patient, I promise you're going to enjoy it.

"Okay bye." A surprise, I liked surprises, but I needed to know where I was going. We drove for ten minutes before I came upon a familiar site. "What the hell . . . the Miami Pier, are we going fishing?" Eden got out of her car and walked to the pier.

"Quincy hurry up." Eden's walk turned into a light skip.

"I'm coming." I replied.

"You can't cum until you're inside me, get over here." She knew exactly what to say to make me want her. We walked down to the end of the pier. We didn't say much to each other. We just held hands. The moon was full and casting a glowing shadow over the calm ocean waters. Eden jumped up on the rail pirouetting.

"Get down before you fall."

"Are you afraid Quincy, are you afraid for me, or are you afraid of me?"

"Just get down, I don't want anything to happen to you."

She did a hand stand and flipped down. Impressive, Eden
was more than impressive. She was in-fucking-credible.
"I need you Quincy, right now." She began to unzip my
slacks forcing her tongue into my mouth. Eden very
aggressively unbuckled my belt. I stood there in my
boxers, with my slacks around my ankles. She grabbed
my underwear by the waist band and snatched. She
snatched again, I couldn't believe she just ripped off my
silk draws.
"Wait baby, what if someone comes," I said.
"Fuck them, you just worry about fucking me." Eden bent
down in a squat sucking on me. After a few licks, I was as
hard as a brick. She put all of me in her mouth. I thought
she was going to swallow it. I noticed that she was finger-
ing herself. Sucking and stroking, jacking and sucking.
She gave the best brain combination.
"Suck it baby . . . suck it." I whispered softly.
"Shut up, don't say shit," she said. Eden stood up pulling
me towards her. I picked her up, placing her on the rail of
the pier. She had on a skin tight mini with no panties.
While I kissed her legs, she pulled her skirt up exposing
her vagina. The moon reflected the moisture that was
coming from her body.
"Eat it Quincy . . . taste me." I wanted to eat it, I really
did. I decided to just put my meat in her instead of my

tongue.

"You like that, that's what you want?" I asked moving in and out of her slowly. She was looking at me with an empty stare.

"Stop Quincy . . . stop." She pushed me away.

"What's wrong, am I hurting you?"

"No baby, it feels real good. I stopped you because I want your tongue in me, I want you to taste me. Eat me baby, eat me." I put my face in it, licking up and down, in and out. I was sucking slowly while putting my forefinger in her, she grabbed my ears and the back of my head hunching my face.

"Ohhhh . . . Quincy, you're . . . making me . . . " She was shaking all over squeezing my head.

"Put it in me . . . get it baby, get it." She was yelling how good it felt, I was so excited and caught up in Eden I came quick. It's all good, we both got ours. I stood there inside her. We kissed and repeated our actions.

"I really missed you baby, I missed you being inside me. Don't ever stay away from me that long again. Promise me Quincy, promise me."

"I promise, I'll always be here."

•   •   •   •   •   •

The next day I was feeling good. I was still a little pissed at Alexis for ruining my clothes and slashing the tires. She had the truck tires repaired and was working on my new wardrobe. It was the first of the month, time to get paid. All of my commission checks came on the first, but there appeared to be a slight problem.

"Alexis . . . how do you spend all the money I give you? I know that we have bills and the kids, but this is ridiculous." I was looking at the statements from the bank trying to add up the numbers.

"Three cars, a truck, a motorcycle, and this big ass over priced house we live in is what I spend money on. Besides, I need to get a part time job just to feed your big ass. Don't ask me what I spend money on, you need to check yourself. Spending all our money in the club buying the bar for the boys. You ain't got to set it out for them all the time, they using you."

"I just asked a simple question, I didn't need all that extra lip, I'm just saying, I'm looking at the numbers and you're spending excessive amounts of money, check yourself."

"Ain't this a bitch, all these years you wined and dined me now you cry broke?"

"I'm not crying broke, you're just spending too much money."

"You're the one who always told me to buy the best. Now you want me to eat hamburger, when I'm accustomed to steak. Please . . . you better get out there and make that money," she said sarcastically snapping her finger.

"Who are you talking to . . . who you talking to? I made you. When I met you, you were trying to get from under the wings of your controlling parents. You didn't have shit, didn't know shit, and wasn't going to be shit. How can you fix your mouth to say that to me?

I tell you what . . . I'm out!"

"Justin where are you going, don't leave," she said in a panic.

"I'm out."

My life was a hole. A hole full of possibilities and unknowns, amerced in lies, deceit, deception and sex. Everything was a lie. I was a liar, cheat, and heartbreaker. Yet I made no attempt to try and relieve myself from this misery. I believed I was crazy, crazy because what brought me discomfort also brought me joy. We had a fight every three months, it was just like clock work. Relationship maintenance is what I called it, only this time I was really pissed.

Chapter Twelve
Sixty-Nine

69 . . . ringing . . .

"Hello."

"Eden, its Quincy."

"Yes Quincy."

"I need you."

"Come where I am, I'm here for you."

"I'm not sure if you know what I mean."

"Tell me."

"I don't know what direction my life is going. I just had a fight with my wife. I feel as if I need help, but I don't know who can help me, I just need you right now."

"I hear you baby, I can feel your pain. I'm here for you, just come."

"I'm coming baby."

Standard operating procedure, always call your main lady after your wife has pissed you off. You're always more sensitive and attentive to their needs during this time. The other woman usually will treat you like a king. They feel this is prime time to gain ground on the wife. The only thing is that I'm not up to no good this time, this time it was real.

Eden greeted me immediately, "Hi baby."

"Hi." We kissed and embraced. I held Eden tightly in my arms. I could feel my emotions passing through her.

"Come lay down."

The mood was soft and subdued. I laid on my stomach looking out at the ocean. My mind was at peace. I felt a since of comfort there. Eden straddled me, she began to massage my lower back. That's just what I needed.

"Go to sleep baby, I'll be here when you wake up . . . go to sleep." I closed my eyes. Eden caressed my back as I drifted off to sleep. I was awakened about an hour later by muffled chatter. Eden was talking to someone on the phone.

"I'm going to be tied up all day. I'm going to have to cancel." She paused, there was a moment of silence. "Don't act like that, I'm all yours. I'll call you later . . .

bye."

Eden entered the room.

"Quincy." She called my name rubbing my back. I pretended as if she had just awakened me.

"Yes baby."

"Are you okay? You've been sleep for an hour."

"I'm fine, just tired, I have a lot of things going on."

"Well if you want to talk I'll listen."

"I've been having a lot of problems at home. Even though I caused most of them, I'm just fed up with the situation. My wife is good to me, don't get me wrong, she's wonderful. Wonderful for someone else, not me, I like to play."

"What do you mean play?"

"I like to play around."

"So, are you playing with me Quincy?"

"No, I'm not saying that. I do have feelings for you that I have never had for any other woman. I know that might sound crazy, even typical, but that's the way I feel."

"It doesn't sound crazy to me baby. I have feelings for you too. Strong feelings, but I have someone else. I don't know if I'm willing to trade in my life for you. I like to play too. Let's just enjoy the time we spend together. I don't think it's healthy for us to continue this conversation. Just enjoy me Quincy, enjoy me and make love to me baby."

"I feel you baby. I'm just going through something." I
said.

"Well, I'm here for you."

I guess I'd be going back to Alexis after all. Not
by choice, but by default. Eden quickly stated, " I know
what will cheer you up." I thought we were about to make
love. I sat up in the bed and began taking off my shirt.
"What are you doing?" Eden asked smiling at me.

"We're not going to make love, we're going yachting."

"You have a yacht?"

"Yes, I love the ocean. We're going to Bimini for lunch.
Put your shirt back on you silly goose." I stood up with an
astonished look on my face, not sure how to deal with this
new experience. Eden claimed she just wanted us to enjoy
each other, but it seemed she was doing everything to pull
me from Alexis. I don't know, maybe I was reading too
much into this, maybe this was just how she rolled.

"So how long does it take to get there?" I asked.

"Not long, it should take us about an hour. Come on, let's
go," she replied eagerly. We left the condo and walked to
the dock.

The yacht was magnificent. It was 42 feet in
length, with a master state room and a cedar lined floor.
The yacht also had a main salon, guest cabin, full bar, and
galley. I estimated the cost at about 500,000 dollars.

"Eden how do you pay for all of this?" I asked inquisitively. She responded fast and stern, "I don't!" I didn't ask anymore questions about the yacht, the condo, or the Benz. Her response answered all my questions. I decided then I would sit back and enjoy the luxuries she obviously received from other men. I knew then what she was about. I'll be damn if I was going to buy her another car, ring, or boat. I'm nobodies Sugar Daddy.

"What are you thinking about?" She asked.

"I'm thinking about you, about the mysterious Eden."

"Don't get scared now, I don't want anything from you Quincy, just your company."

"I understand that, but my concern is for me."

"What do you mean?"

"Someone is taking very good care of you, look at all this. Men that spend money like this will do anything to protect it. So what I'm saying is don't put me in a situation where I'm confronted by your man, because I won't hesitate."

"What, you a killer now?"

"No. I'm no killer, but I won't hesitate." She leaned back with a smirk on her face putting her shades upon her delicate face.

"Calm down Rambo, I wouldn't put myself in that position. I can handle my end, you just keep your shit straight."

"My shit stay tight, I got mine." I said. I felt like an asshole, because I just told her I had problems at home. "We'll see." She started the boat up and we made the fifty mile trip to Bimini.

The place was beautiful. The water was crystal clear. The area had blue lagoons and water falls. I've often heard of it's sunsets, sand, pristine waters, reefs, and superb fishing. It was plain to see why Eden loved the ocean.

"Quincy, lets go for a swim."

I wanted to say, "*A swim, the water is at least 25 feet deep, full of fish and other shit that can eat you, I don't think so!*" But I remained tough.

"What happened to lunch, I thought we were going to eat?" I said in an attempt to keep myself out of the water. "You can eat all you want baby." Eden took off her swim suit, she turned to allow me to see her naked body. "Come get your lunch." She jumped into the water. I began taking off my clothes so fast I tripped and nearly fell over board. I did a back flip into the water. "I didn't know you could do that Quincy." "I can do a lot, come here."

Eden swam over to me, we were holding each other treading water while we kissed. I took a deep breath, went under water, and gave her what she wanted.

She was holding my head next to her body while she was spread eagle. I blew bubbles out of my mouth on her body while she sat on my face. I knew that she liked it because she was squeezing my head. I had to come up, my air supply was gone. I stopped and tried to return to the surface. I couldn't because she was holding my head with her legs wrapped around my neck. I pushed Eden away and exploded to the surface.

"What the hell?" I could barely breathe, let alone talk. "What are you doing, are you trying to kill me?" I said angrily while coughing. Eden looked at me, turned and swam back to the boat. I followed her, yelling for her to answer me. We climbed on the yacht, standing face to face.

"Answer me Eden," I yelled grabbing her shoulders.

"I was climaxing Quincy, it felt so good I just got caught up." They say sex can kill you. I just didn't think I would be a victim.

"Caught up, you almost killed me."

"I'm sorry, I didn't mean to hurt you." I looked at her naked body glistening from the sun rays reflecting off the water.

"It's okay, let's go down below." Eden looked up showing all 32. She grabbed my hand leading me below deck where we laid as one.

• • • • • •

"Did you like it baby?"

"I loved it Quincy. I love your big thing inside me, it's a nice change." Change, change from what I thought to myself. At that time my cell rang, it was Alexis.

"Hello."

"Justin?"

"Yes, Baby." I could hear the pain in her voice.

"Come home baby."

"I'll be there shortly." I hung up the cell phone looking at Eden.

"Time to go." She said.

"Yeah baby, time to go."

We got dressed and returned to the deck of the yacht. We rode all the way to Bimini and the only thing I ate was Eden. I was still hungry. I wondered what she meant by it's a nice change. I thought about that all the way back to Miami. The answer to my question was standing right in front of me. Fear of what she might say kept me from asking her to explain. I learned a lot about Eden that day. Maybe too much.

"Quincy look at the moon." I paused and looked at the moon shining brighter than any of the stars.

"Yeah, it's beautiful." I responded after taking a long

stare. "What's wrong with you?" Asked Eden.

It's a full moon and I'm a werewolf.

"Oh nothing, just enjoying the ride." We could see the city lights from the water. Everything looked so peaceful. We arrived at the dock behind Eden's condo.

"Grab the rope and tie it off," Eden said. Wanting me to tie the yacht to the dock. *Who did she think I was, Gilligan?*

"Thanks for a great time. I really enjoyed myself, despite the fact you almost killed me." I said reaching for her.

"I'm sorry, I enjoyed you also. So, when will I see you again?" She asked as we embraced.

"You might see me later tonight if things don't work out with my wife." I said taking in a deep breath. I jumped off the boat.

"Make it work." Eden replied.

"I'll give you a call later."

As I walked off from Eden, I looked up at the high rise she lived in. Then looked back at her and the yacht. She was living a playboy's dream. I thought I was a player. I'm nothing compared to her, definitely not a player. Her life-style was on an entirely different level. Well, it was time for Justin to emerge. During the ride home I anticipated what might happen at home. I didn't know, but if it was going down, I was ready to get it over with.

Chapter Thirteen
Pain Is Just A Feeling

"Alexis?" I yelled out loudly. All the lights were off in the house which was very unusual.

"Up here." A shout came from upstairs.

"Why are all the lights off?" I asked switching the lights on.

"Come up here. Come up here now!" Alexis yelled in a stuttering voice.

"Where have you been?" I looked at her not believing what I saw. "Where have you been?" She yelled out repeatedly. Alexis was drunk and stumbling about.

"Don't say you were with your friends, I called them no good bastards. Yeah, don't look surprised, I called them and none of them knew where you were." Alexis was standing in front of me in the dimly lit room swaying back and forth like a small tree in a storm.

"Justin, answer me!"

"Honey, calm down"

"Calm!" She yelled out sputtering her partly swallowed drink. "Don't try and pacify me, I ain't calming down a damn thing," Alexis said as she stumbled in my direction.

"Honey, let's sit and talk."

"Fuck that, you think we can talk then you fuck me and everything is all right? You can't keep hurting me Justin, you can't keep hurting me."

Alexis was stumbling about the room crying. After seeing my reaction to her drunken state, she began to regain control of her emotions.

"I don't want to hurt you baby . . . stop crying, please don't cry," I said calmly holding her in my arms.

"You're wrong, you're wrong."

"Wrong about what?" I was confused about what she was referring to. She yelled in an uncontrollable outburst, pushing me away.

"I can smell her on you . . . I can smell your bitches scent on you!" She started kicking and screaming, "I hate you." Alexis hit me, crying and cursing. She eventually tired and fell to her knees, repeating one simple question, "why . . . why . . . why?" I picked my wife up off the floor and laid her on the bed. I laid next to her looking at her puffy, swollen eyes. I wiped a single tear from her face as she took in a deep breath.

"You can't keep hurting me like this, you can't keep hurting me." She closed her eyes and fell asleep.

Looking at Alexis, I thought about the woman I married. The woman that laid there was not her. I was told if someone can take something away from you it's not yours. Alexis often told me I took her self respect and esteem. In her fits of rage she told me she married the wrong man, constantly reminding me of her background. Alexis' parents didn't approve of their daughter being married to a ghetto thug who just happened to have money. I didn't care, in some strange way I wish she had listened to them. I think their disapproving of me so adamantly only made me want their daughter even more. I wasn't supposed to be in this marriage. We weren't supposed to be in this marriage. The only reason we were together was to prove her family was not right about me. Once the vacations and the sex was done, and it was just Alexis and I alone with these four walls, we both knew this wasn't meant to be. We loved each other, but I don't think we liked one another. I was nice to her when I messed over her, and mean to her when I didn't. She didn't deserve this, I didn't deserve this.

I laid there for several hours, watching her, thinking of all the things I could do to make what she obviously knew better. In all the things running through my mind, I couldn't think of one thing that would make the situation better. Any lie would have only made matters worse. How would I tell the mother of my children I wanted out of the marriage? I decided not to tell her. I swallowed my feelings, accepted I was wrong, and prayed she would forgive me again. That wasn't the best thing for me, but it was the best thing for us.

•   •   •   •   •   •

"Good morning darling, how are you?" Alexis sat up in bed, holding her head. She looked at me in a disgusted manner. "How are you feeling?" I asked again.
"You asked me that once, you don't have to keep asking."
"I'm just trying . . ." Alexis interrupted me.
"I know, you're always trying, trying to please everyone but me." She slowly raised her head. "I'm tired of being second in your life. I'm second to your selfish needs. For a long time I thought I was confused, but I realized its not me. I want you to leave. Leave . . . find what ever it is you're searching for." Alexis said looking down, sitting on the edge of the bed.
"You want *me* to leave?" I was thinking this is my house,

you leave.

"Yes, I can't stand to be around you now, just go." She said calmly trying not to cry.

"I'll leave, Alexis I'm sorry."

"Sorry, Sorry . . . you're right, you're a sorry man. Sorry didn't ruin us, you did."

I turned and walked away from my wife. Hurt because I had hurt her. As for my own feelings, I was relieved. Relieved all the years of cheating were exposed. A way out of this situation had been paved. I was relieved she knew I was just a no good man. I stopped, looked back, and asked, "Is our marriage over?" Alexis didn't bother to respond. I walked out of my house, uncertain if I would ever return. I don't know if I cared.

• • • • • •

I got in my car trying to soak up what just happened. At that moment I decided to cut off all my relationships, I knew they were the source of my problems. Besides, I didn't love those ho's.

26 . . . ringing . . .

"Hello?"

"Hi, its Tony."

"Hi baby how are you?"

"I've seen better days. Listen, I'm calling to tell you a couple of things that have been on my mind."

"What's wrong Tony?"

"Well, that's part of the problem, Tony is not my real name. My name is Justin. I've lied to you all this time. I didn't do it to hurt you, I did it because that's the way I used to be."

"Why are you telling me this Justin?"

"I just want to come clean. I'm tired of hurting people. I'm tired of hurting myself."

"You sound as if you're confused about who you really are. You need to find yourself. I hope you find whatever you need." To my surprise she actually seemed concerned about what I was going through.

"Listen baby, I'm calling to say good-bye, I can't keep living like this."

"I know Tony, Justin, whoever you are. I know . . . take care of yourself."

"You do the same." I paused with my ear to the phone as she hung up.

I called all the women I had a relationship with and told them the truth. I cut all of them off. Surprisingly, most of them were understanding. Sandra, my little married freak told me she hoped I got syphilis in my ass and died. I wasn't mad at her. I was her excitement. How dare I up root myself from her life without any warning. I deleted all the stored numbers in my cell phone. All except one.

69 . . . ringing . . .

Eden picked up the phone, "she kicked you out?"

"Yeah, something like that," silence came over the phone.

"You know where I am, if you want to come you can." Eden replied.

"I'm going to drive around for a while. I'll come over in two hours or so. Is that okay?"

"That's fine, I'll see you when you get here."

"Okay, I'll see you soon. Thanks baby."

"Thank me later."

"Okay."

"Bye."

"Bye baby."

   I was riding on the expressway thinking what I was doing couldn't be more wrong. Why was everything that's so wrong felt so good? I knew that I'd hurt Alexis, not to mention the kids. What kind of father was I? The worse kind I guess. Living a life of lies wasn't cool anymore. A single man's life was not the life for me, but I'd been living this way since I was a teenager. Pimpin' ho's,

managi trois, living large in the eyes of friends. It's all
petty.

I pulled over to the side of the road to vomit. I was
sick. Sick of myself. I looked in the mirror and yelled
out, "I'm sick of you!" I yelled out to relieve myself of the
stress. It was years of frustration and cowardly acts
clogged up inside me. I had been lying for so long that I
had began to believe my own drama. The drama that was
once my fuel, my purpose for living now sickened me. I
was at the back of my car spewing my guts out.

"Excuse me sir, do you need assistance?" I looked up
slowly, wiping the slob from my chin. It was the police.
"Sir, are you okay? Have you been drinking?" Drinking,
hell no I hadn't been drinking. I needed a drink. I guess
they assumed I had been drinking because I was vomiting.
"No sir, I haven't been drinking, I'm car sick."
"Have you traveled a great distance?" Asked the officer.
"No." I said standing firmly looking at the cops.
"I need to see your drivers licence and registration sir."
"For what, I wasn't driving." I responded with a raised
brow.
"Licence and registration sir."

One of the officers was directly in front of me.
The other had positioned himself off my right flank. I
could tell they just wanted to harass me. A black man in a

convertible XK8. They probably thought I stole it or I was a drug dealer.

"Here's my drivers license, the registration is in the glove compartment."

"Do you mind if I retrieve your registration Mr. Drake?" The officer said looking down at my drivers license.

"Yes I do mind. If you would allow me I'll get it for you." The officer watched my every move as I leaned to open the glove compartment to retrieve the car's registration.

"Is this your vehicle sir?"

"What kind of question is that? Of course its my car."

"Just answer the question."

"This is bullshit!"

"Sir, I'm going to administer a field sobriety test. I believe that you've been driving under the influence."

"I haven't been drinking. You think I'm drunk? I'm not drunk, and I'm not taking any field test!"

"Sir, are you refusing to comply?"

"You fucking right, fuck you and fuck your test!"

"Sir, put your hands on the car."

"What?"

"Put your hands on the car!" The cop shouted loudly.

"For what?"

"You're under arrest."

"Under arrest, you're not arresting me. Arresting me for

what?" Other cops arrived on the scene. I saw the situation about to explode. I backed away from the officers as they advanced towards me. "What am I being arrested for? I've done nothing wrong." I said as I backed away.

One of the officers rushed me. I heard other voices yelling, "take him to the ground, take him to the ground." I began to violently resist. All the stuff I was going through, these cops had no idea. I had a lot of anger inside and I was mad at myself, so I didn't care what happened. I was willing to die that day. I began to throw the officers off. I yelled out, "bring it, bring it pigs." I clutched my fist and fired on the first one that came into striking distance. I was throwing my fist fast and as hard as I could. My intentions were lethal. I was swinging wildly while backing up. I was punching myself out, fatigue had overcome me, and all the blows I'd taken began to take a toll on me. I grabbed one of the officers in a head lock and fell to the ground with him. I figured if they were going to do this to me, I was going to kill at least one of them. While on the ground I was being kicked and pelted with knight sticks. I released the cop and balled up in a fetal position to protect myself. The last thing I remembered was hearing the cops say "treat him like a King." I knew exactly what that meant.

I woke up beaten and bruised, handcuffed in the

back of the police car. I rubbed my tongue across my
teeth to check if any were missing. Soft ass pigs, that's
what they live for, to beat brothers down.

The cop opened the back door of the squad car. "Mr.
Drake, you have the right to remain silent, anything you
say can and will be used against you in a court of law. If
you cannot afford an attorney, one will be provided for
you."

"Yeah, Yeah, I understand. Why did you arrest me?"

"You were placed under arrest for refusing to take a field
sobriety test, that's against the law."

"What? I'm not drunk."

"Yeah, whatever, tell it to the Judge," he closed the door.
They all stood there looking at me and my drivers licence.
I'm sure they noticed the address. All the cops had that
"we fucked up" look on their face.

"Put the top up on my car!" I yelled out from the back of
the hot patrol car. One cop came over and opened the
door.

"What did you say sir?"

"Put the top up on my car!"

"Your car is going to be towed to the police impound yard,
besides you don't need to worry about your car, worry
about your ass!"

"There's no reason to tow my car. My car ain't got noth-

ing to do with this. Just put the top up, roll the windows
up, and I'll have it picked up."

"Sir, your car is being impounded for refusing the sobriety
test. That warrants us towing your car. We handle these
situations as if you were a drunk driver. You can have
someone pick it up from the impound yard." The cop
slammed the door.

"Just roll up my fucking windows and put the top up!"

It was a long ride to the police station. Arrested,
arrested over some bullshit. I knew I would beat this, but
what effect will this have on my career? What about
Alexis? What about my kids? This was really a fucked
up day. We arrived at the station.

"Step out of the car sir and watch your head." Stepping
out of the car I winced from the pain. The adrenaline rush
had worn off, and the pain of the beating was starting to
materialize. I limped through a metal door into the pro-
cessing center. My handcuffs were not removed because I
had resisted the cops.

"Now what?" I asked.

"You're going to be given a breathalyzer test to determine
your bodies alcohol content."

"Let's do it." I was eager because I wasn't drunk, I was
eager to prove my innocence. I blew into the machine. It
was painful because my lips and jaw were swollen.

"Blow," said the officer. I leaned back looking up at the ceiling. The cuffs were irritating my wrist.

"You didn't blow long enough Mr. Drake. You need to lean forward, put your mouth on the apparatus, and blow until I tell you to stop. Are you ready?" I nodded my head yes.

"Blow." I blew as hard as I could. "Stop." The cop looked at the machine and then looked at me.

"What's the results?" I said sarcastically.

"According to the Breathalyzer, you're— " he paused looking back at the machine.

"I'm what?" He shifted in the chair and leaned back. "According to the breathalyzer you're not under the influence."

"I'd like my phone call officer."

I was going to try to nail these fucks to the wall. I had one of the top lawyers in the country. He was not Johnny, but he would eat this up. They put me in a holding cell with a bunch of drunks. Man was not meant to be imprisoned. I definitely wasn't built for this shit. I sat in that cold cell on the floor four hours looking at the men that were there. Not knowing any of their backgrounds, I could see myself in each of them. We all had a look of disbelief and confusion.

"Justin Drake," a voice yelled. "Check out time," said the

guard. I walked out of the cell looking back promising myself never to return. I saw my lawyer Bernie standing on the other side of a glass partition. His mouth open, surprised to see me in that condition.

"What happened?" My lawyer asked.

"I got my ass kicked."

"Are you okay?" He asked placing his hand on my shoulder.

"I'm okay . . . my ostrich boots are ruined, but besides that I'm okay."

"We're going to sue. The police officers, the city, everybody." Bernie was enraged, he looked at all the cops in the station.

"What about my car?" I asked.

"It's fine, its in the parking lot." We walked out of the station.

"Handle this Bernie, handle this."

"I will, don't worry, its done. Are you going to be okay?"

"Yeah, I'm fine," I limped down the steps to my car. "Yo Bernie."

"Yeah." He said swinging around.

"Don't tell Alexis."

Chapter Fourteen
The Garden Of Eden

In the still of night,
Fear is vibrant.
Listening for the first scream,
Fear is only rivaled by
death, the conqueror of fear.
Once death is not feared,
fear does not exist.

— *M. Gainer*

69 ringing . . . ringing . . . ringing . . .

"Hello you've reached Eden, I'm not available. Please leave a detailed message at the tone . . .

Beeeeeeeeeeeeeep."

"I don't know if your machine can hold all the details.

You know who it is, call me when you get a minute."

"Hello, Hello."

"Hi, are you screening your calls now?" I said sounding like I had just come from the dentist.

"No, I was in the shower . . . what happened to you, I thought you were coming over earlier?"

"I'll tell you when I get there. I'm on my way."

"Okay baby."

"Okay then, bye." I should've went home, maybe Alexis would have felt sorry for me. I doubt it, she'd probably be happy I got my ass beat. She's wanted to kick my ass for years. I walked through the lobby of Eden's condo, everyone was staring, moving to the side, women clutching their handbags. I heard one guy say, "damn, he's fucked up." Only if he knew, I felt worse than I looked. I stepped in the elevator alone, looking at all the images of myself staring back. "Damn, I am fucked up," I said looking in the mirrors on the elevator. I reached the 35th floor, *Paradise*.

"Eden, Daddy's home."

"Hey Daddy," she said, not yet seeing me. I walked to the kitchen to get some ice for my face. I ripped the rest of what once was a nice shirt off and used it for a compress.

"Are you making yourself a drink?" Eden asked after hearing the ice maker.

"No."

"Then what are you doing?" I could hear footsteps coming towards me. I was sitting on the counter with my back to her. "What are you doing?" She asked as she rounded the corner.

"Oh my God! Baby what happened to you?" She grabbed me and started to cry. "What happened, what happened?" Eden said trembling.

"On my way over here I got pulled over by the cops. I refused a sobriety test and this is the result." I held my hands out to my side so she could see my battered body.

"Oh my God, Quincy are you okay?"

"I'll be okay, I'm just sore." Eden took the ice pack from me and gently placed it on my jaw. She kissed me on my chest, saying that she was sorry that I had experienced such a thing. She led me to the bathroom.

"Take off your clothes baby, a warm bath will make you feel better." In the bathroom, I could really see the extent of my injuries. I was practically black and blue from head to toe! Eden had this big ass hot tub, that was just the thing I needed. As I looked in the mirror, I saw Eden standing behind me holding her hands over her eyes.

"What's wrong?" I asked.

"Your back, your back."

"It's okay baby . . . it's okay." I grabbed and hugged her.

I could imagine what my back must look like. When I balled up to protect myself my back took most of the abuse.

"Run the water for me." Eden walked over to the tub slowly and turned on the water, pouring oils in as well. "This will make you feel better baby." I stepped into the tub trying to appear tough, when I really wanted to cry like a punk. The warm water felt as if it were 1000 degrees. I sat down, extended my body, and relaxed.

"Thank you." I said softly to Eden.

"For what?" Eden asked with tearful eyes.

"Thanks for being here for me." Eden stood up looking down at my battered face. She took off her clothes and got in the tub with me. She straddled me, holding my face with her small, soft hands. She grabbed the sponge and gently began to wash my body. She washed my face, neck, and upper torso. She stood up repositioning herself.

"I'm not hurting you am I?"

"No baby, it feels good." Eden rubbed the sponge across my chest down to my groin.

"Quincy, you're hard . . . your thing is hard!"

"I'm hurt, not dead." I replied. We both laughed in unison.

"You're in no condition to handle this. Relax, relax, when you're better I'll give you some."

"I can live with that. In the mean time, do something for me to make me feel better."

"Like what?" She asked smiling.

"Show me something." Eden began to rub and fondle her breast. She sat on the edge of the tub facing me. She grabbed the oil and poured it over her body. She spread her legs raising her knees, rubbing on her vagina. She opened herself so I could see into her pink tunnel of love.

"How many fingers can you take?" I asked to influence her actions. She inserted one finger inside, moving in and out, then two fingers, then three. Eden leaned her head back enjoying the way she was feeling.

"Make yourself feel good baby." I could tell she was excited, her clitoris was swollen.

"Do it baby, do it." I raised my foot out of the tub and put my big toe in her. She jirated her pelvis, holding on to the tub with four of my toes inside of her. I removed my foot and she slipped slowly back into the tub, looking at me with half opened eyes.

"Are you okay?" I asked her.

"Ahh— I'm fine." I stood up and stepped out of the tub drying myself looking at Eden.

"Go lay down baby, I'm coming," She said. I limped to the bedroom, reflecting on the days events. *I should write a book about this.* I sat on the edge of the bed and looked out at the ocean. Eden entered the room.

"Put your feet in the bed." She lifted my feet and placed them down softly.

"You like my feet, huh?" I asked.

"I love your feet." She laid down besides me with her head on my chest.

"What are you going to do Quincy?"

"About what?" I asked.

"About everything."

"I'm going to live . . . I'm going to live." We fell asleep.

• • • • • •

"Wake up, Wake up! Get your clothes, get up, get up." Eden yelled frantically.

"What?" I said a bit disoriented.

"Get yo shit!"

"What's wrong?"

"My people are here." I heard the elevator doors close.

"Get in the closet, get in the closet." I scooped up all of my belongings and ran to hide in the closet. Under normal conditions I would have went out the window or out the back door, or told that cat to check his woman, cause she choose me. But, I was 35 stories up. I didn't need this.

While in the closet, I heard loud screams and cursing. "Who you got in here bitch, who you got in my shit?" A voice yelled out.

"Calm down baby," replied Eden.

"Who's in here?"

I peaked through a crack, trying to make out the images. My heart was beating fast. I was too hurt to fight or run. Hold up, that sounds like a woman's voice! At that very moment, the closet doors flew open, I was looking down the barrel of a chrome 45.

Chapter Fifteen
Dumb Ass Me

I wasn't going out like this. Butt naked, beaten
and bruised in a closet. All my dreams and hopes were
over. What about my children? I'd never get the chance
to see them grow up. I closed my eyes and accepted what
was about to happen. I decided pride was no longer an
issue. If given the chance, I would beg for my life, and if I
lived, I would ask God for forgiveness.

"Justin!" A voice said angrily. I opened my eyes.
"Alexis?"

Alexis asked quickly, "What are you doing here?"

Eden asked, "Who is Justin? What's happening?" Eden
was yelling loudly at this point.

Alexis turned to Eden, "What the fuck is he doing here?"

I asked Alexis to put the gun down.

Alexis yelled to me, "Shut up!"

Eden yelled again, "what's happening?" Eden was confused.

"This is my husband. You're fucking him and me?"

"I didn't know."

"What, Alexis you're a dyke, you're sleeping with Eden?"

"Yeah, I'm sleeping with her. We've been fucking for three years," she said pointing the gun at Eden.

Alexis then turned to Eden, "after all these years, after all the things I gave you, the condo, the cars, the yacht. This is how you repay me!" Alexis said with clutched teeth.

I was now the one confused. "Alexis, you bought all of this?"

"No, you dumb bastard. Actually *YOU* bought all of this. I bought it with *your* money. You wanted to know what I spend our money on, I spent it on this trick."

Eden screamed, "I didn't know . . . I didn't know." Eden was now trembling, unable to control herself.

"Shut up bitch." Alexis slapped Eden with the butt of the gun. Eden fell to her knees clutching her face.

"I told you not to fuck over me!" Alexis said kicking Eden with her stiletto heels.

"Put the gun down baby, put the gun down." Alexis looked at me as if she had a bad taste in her mouth.

"Baby, if I was your baby you wouldn't be up here with

my woman. I knew you wasn't shit when I married your ass. All these years coming home smelling like other women. I should have killed your ass a long time ago," she said cocking back the hammer on the gun.

"What about the kids, think about our children."

"The kids, you don't care about the kids, you're just trying to save your ass."

Eden managed to look up from the floor, "Alexis I'm sorry, I never meant to hurt you."

"Fuck yo life!" Alexis fired a single shot hitting Eden in the head.

"NO!" I screamed in pain for Eden as Alexis spit on her and looked up at me.

"Shut up, shut the hell up," she said to me.

"You're crazy, what have you done?"

"I'm crazy Justin? You think I'm crazy. If I'm crazy, you made me this way. All the years knowing you were cheating on me made me this way. All I ever wanted was your love. That's all I ever wanted was for you to want me, just me."

"Alexis, put the gun down, we can work this out."

"Work it out? It's over. My life is over, you killed me a long time ago with your lies."

Alexis put the gun in her mouth and pulled the trigger.

"NOOOO!" I ran over to my wife's lifeless body, raising

her slowly from the marble floors. As I held her, I could
hear her faint gasps for air. She was still alive.

"Hold on baby, hold on," I told her covering the hole in
the back of her head. She held on to me tightly, raising
her arm, placing her hand on the back of my neck, pulling
me towards her mouth. I bent down slowly to hear her last
words.

"Yes baby, what is it?"

"F-U-C-K You!" With her other hand she raised the gun
to my head and pulled the trigger.

"Click . . . click." The gun jammed. Alexis' body went
limp and the gun fell to the floor.

Chapter Sixteen
The Dead Are Concious Of Nothing

As I sat in that closet, looking at two people I cared dearly for sprawled over the floor, I couldn't help but think about the past 2,016 hours of my life. In my desperate search for happiness, I managed to eliminate all that really mattered in my world. Funny how my world managed to hurt so many people. I suppose my selfishness was contagious, because it spread to Alexis and Eden like an infectious disease.

Then again, maybe I'm being too harsh on myself. After all, Alexis pursued me like a poacher on a rare white tiger. Perhaps I was a victim of her wants and desires. As for Eden, she was just another prey in the Congo, befriending anyone who could satisfy her acquired taste.

After all these years, I would have never thought that Alexis would have done this to me. Looking back, that's exactly why she did it, she knew I would have never suspected it. The yacht, the condo, and all the beautiful things Eden owned I purchased. Well, my wife purchased with my money. Never in a million years would I have thought that either of them were bisexual. Life's a bitch.

I was left there to reflect on the things I'd done. Left to deal with my feelings, the consequences of my actions. My children, what about them? How was I to explain that their mother was dead. I thought I was willing to pay any price to live a playboy's life-style. I knew some things didn't have any monetary value. What can I say, *Dumb Ass Me.*

I had to somehow put this behind me. I had to go on living, and provide a full life for my children. Over the course of the last three months I've learned I cannot make anyone whole or happy. Each person is responsible for there own destiny. Destiny and fate are not accidents or coincidence, they are groomed for many years. All my years of being a playboy finally paid off. I had to come to the realization that today's events were not coincidental, but consequences of my life style.

I know rehashing the events of the day was not going to ease all the pain I felt and had to explain.

Women always seem to get their way. Alexis and Eden were dead, they were conscious of nothing. Alexis did not have to explain to our kids why she committed suicide. Alexis would not have to explain to her parents why there Prima Donna was now gone. As for Eden, I only knew a pin hole about her life. I had no idea what would result from my relationship with this woman. I suppose all of her secrets left with her. Damn, I had to explain this to Sylvia too. My mother was an understanding woman, lets see how well she'd understand the events of that day.

At that moment I saw the police opening the elevator to my paradise turned hell. It was the same cops who arrested me earlier. This was the first day of the rest of my life.

Ladies, if any of these scenarios look remotely familiar, you're being played! Or, you're a player!

Fellas, if this is how you roll, congratulations! You're playing the game.

For those who are watching, if you ever decide to dive in, these are tried and true rules of the game. Proceed with caution!

Tips Of The Pimpin' Trade

1. **Fully Clean**. If you shower be sure to use a non deodorant soap. If you must shower with a deodorant soap, wash your genital area only. Wash your genitals with the *soap* and the rest of your body with water and a soap free bath rag. If time does not permit for a shower, stop at the store, buy a single beer, use the beer as body wash. I know this sounds crazy. Trust me, this will masquerade the scent of sex. The beer will also cover the odor of the deodorant soap. Splash the beer on your face and arms, pack it on heavy. Next, pour a little of the beer in

your hands, rub it on your genital's area. Not too much though, you don't want to look like you had an accident. When you arrive home play drunk. This will be believed because you smell as such. If you are a non drinker coffee does the same trick. Allow yourself enough time for the coffee to cool, remember to walk in with your drink. Women always smell nice, so ladies, just keep doing what you do. Body spray will do nicely also.

2. ***Don't come home ashy.*** That is a dead give away that you have taken a shower, unless you are just leaving the gym. If you are using the gym as an excuse to see your lover, keep your gym membership current and make sure you lift every now and then so your significant other will see some results. Also, don't use a lotion that you don't have at home. Remember, lotion is scented.

3. ***Loose Lips Sink Ships.*** Tell none of your friends your business. This is the first way to get caught. Involve yourself in activities that don't involve someone else. Get in the habit of doing things alone so when you leave and

do solo activities it won't be suspicious (i.e. gym, gun range, motorcycle riding, walking the dog, golfing, fishing, shopping, book club, hair stylist, etc.)

4. ***Throw it Back***. Never date one of your mates friends. First of all, this person is more scandalous than you. If they want to screw you, they want to screw you over. There is more than one fish in the sea, throw that one back.

5. ***Lay the Pipe***. Spend time at home with the family. Do everything you can imagine physically, emotionally, and most of all sexually. Never be too tired to make love even if you have put on a clinic at the other person's house.

6. ***It Doesn't Matter***. Tell everyone you are involved with you have someone. Make sure they are clear on that fact. If they want you, it won't matter. More than likely it will be a plus.

7. ***Trust Your Gut***. Know when you are in over your head. I can't tell you when this is, but it's a feeling you will have in your gut. Abandon ship when this happens.

How tactful you do this will determine what will happen next.

8. ***Thanks But No Thanks.*** Choose your extra relationships wisely. If they are known stalkers, pass on them. Don't create or look for a problem. An extra marital affair or relationship will be difficult enough to manage without having a crazed lunatic following you.

9. ***Hungry?*** A hungry dog hunts better, a horny dog will make a mistake. Have a hunger for the person, not the sex. The sex will come, be patient.

10. ***School Is In.*** Don't spend your money (at least not all of it). I know you wonder how you're going to do this. I'm going to tell you.

Instructions: If you have the misfortune of dating multiple people and you are not a *Baller* this could cause a problem. This is how you overcome this. Your lover will always want to take care of your needs. Use that to your advantage. You must be a creator of situations, nothing major but you must be able to do this. For example, after you have dated, made love, and just took care of all their wants, this is where the game begins. Check this out, arrive not feeling so well. Their natural response is going to be, "what's wrong baby?" Your response will be, "Nothing . . . I just have some things on my mind. It has nothing to do with you or us, just some personal shit I need to take care of." They will respond, "if I can help let me know, I'm here for you." They'll probably say something along those lines. It's all down hill from here. Tell them, "come over here, sit with me, hold me." Sigh a couple of times and stare at the ceiling, wall or window. Now they are burning up to know what the hell is wrong and how can they make it better. They'll say, "are you sure you're okay?" This is when you come with it. "Baby, I've gotten myself into a jam. I need your help." Make sure you stop talking. Allow them to ask or say they will help you. Your mate will probably say, "Is there anything I can do?" You respond, "I don't know if you can help. I need an X amount of dollars." Next, continue to look bizarre by staring out of the window or something. Lastly, they will say one or two things. "I'll give you the money." Or, "I'll get the money for you." This is when you graciously decline but be careful not to talk yourself out of the money. Allow them to insist you take it and then just say okay.

Now that you have the money, what do you do with it? You take your *other people* out with it. Buy them gifts, flowers, get the car repaired or serviced, pay a bill. One month later you can run the same game. Only this time on the person you spent the money on. The game just re-winds. They'll never ask for it back because you're good to them. Your own money stays in your pocket. Be creative, but careful.

11. **Smother Me.** Women, protect yourself. Don't allow anyone to run up in you without protection. Men put on a helmet. It would be hard to explain why you need to go on a penicillin diet.

12. **Anybody Home?** Never go into someone's house

who has a live in. That is the quickest way to die.

13. **Walk The Dog.** If you are just going to get a quickie, tell your significant other you're going to the store or taking the dog for a walk. Have a small dog so it can be carried (like a York Terrier or Chihuahua). Never travel a distance you can't return home within 15 minutes.

14. **Where Do You Live?** Never let a single person (a person that does not have anyone else) know where you live or in what area you live in (unless you want them stopping by). I know they can find out by running your tag or going through your pockets or purse, but don't make it easy for them.

15. **Home Phone.** Never call from your house phone. Never, I don't have to explain.

16. **What are you doing?** Don't do something you wouldn't normally do. If you don't normally go to foot-ball games alone, don't up and say you're going one day out of the blue. Take the family first, then you can go alone. This shit is like playing chess, you just have to set

up your moves.

17. ***Huh!*** Don't ever think your mate doesn't have a clue what's going on. If it comes up, talk about it. Talk calmly and be very attentive. Don't blow up or get mad, this shows guilt. Always remain in control. Defuse any concerns your significant other may be having.

18. ***Yes I am.*** Never ask your mate "Are you cheating on me?" It's a dead give away that **YOU** are!

19. ***Dress the Part.*** Don't just show up wearing something you didn't buy. If you're low maintenance . . . stay that way!

20. ***Enough Said.*** Be wise, know what you know.

COMING SOON . . .
ANOTHER MICHAEL GAINER NOVEL

ONE LIFE NO $EQUEL

ONE LIFE NO $EQUEL

(A PREVIEW...)

Chapter One

In the last days there will be many false prophets. So many people are waiting for their savior. Kevin believed the only thing that would save him was the dope he was slinging. He had loyal customers from lawyers, doctors, and professional athletes to the everyday Joe. He knew he was contributing to their demise, but he believed they were killing themselves. He didn't put a gun to their head and make them snort cocaine. His rationale was some people liked a glass dick in their mouth.

"Were them boys at?" A voice called out. That was just another way of asking who had drugs.

"What you wont?" He said stepping in the direction of the voice. His fist were clutched holding on to his assets.

"Let me get a fifty." Kevin opened his hand and gave the

crack head a fifty rock of cooked cocaine. Damn junkies, he hated it for their families. They get off from work with two weeks of hard earned cash and spend their entire check on drugs and ho's, while their families were at home sitting in the dark, due to the unpaid bills. How could a man allow his child to wear shitty diapers? Kevin had a real problem with that. He didn't feel sorry for them, he had a family to take care of.

"Were them boys at?"

"What you need fool?"

"Let me get a dove." The man gave Kevin the money. It took him a minute to unravel it all. The money was all balled up.

"Hold up . . . this three dollars!" Kevin yelled to the addict. The baser took off in a dead sprint. Kevin pulled out his gun and took aim, he started to shoot that fool but that would have made the spot hot. He couldn't do that, he was selling more birds than a pet shop. He didn't need the cops messing up his hustle. He decided it was best to deal with that fool later. He knew it was time for him to get off the streets. He was an En-tro-pro-NEGRO that loved having his own money, but the dope game was getting too dangerous.

"Yo G, you should've blast that fool." Clyde his home boy said, raising his shirt showing his stub nose .357.

"I'll deal with that dick sucker later."

"Yo G, you can't let that baser try you like that! You look
bad in front of the boys. You got to deal with that fool so
them other junkies don't try you. Handle your business
Buddy, handle your business." Clyde pimped off down
the street.

Kevin observed the other street hustlers looking at
him shaking their heads. He knew what they were thinking, he was getting soft. "Soft, okay try me like a punk!"
He knew they wanted his spot. He was the only indepen-
dent hustler out there. The rest of those clowns worked
for someone else. He didn't see it, this was a $5K a week
spot and he wasn't going to give the next man $4,000 and
keep a grand for himself. Shit! He just couldn't see it.

Lately the weather had been real nasty. It looked
as if it might rain that night, most of those cats would
leave once the sky opened up. Kevin wasn't going any
place. It could have been a deluge. He would just build
an ark.

"What they do?" A voice called out, from the shadows of
the ally.

"What's up fool?"

"You holding?"

"Holding? Holding?" What type of question was that?
Kevin thought to himself.

"I don't sell drugs officer." He replied with a smile on his face.

"Shut your mouth boy! I'll bust your ass right now!" The under cover cop said, standing chest to chest with Kevin.

"Do what you gotta do, I ain't got nothing on me." Kevin said holding his arms out by his side. The cop walked off. It was time for Kevin to dip, but before he left.

"Five O, Po-Po in the hole!" He yelled before running trough a wooded area. Them other dealers probably wouldn't have said shit, but he thought he'd save at least one of them from going to jail. He stopped running for a split second to look back. Those cats were scattering and running about like roaches with the lights on. Kevin saw the cop look back at him, but the cop knew what time it was. He'd need a rocket in his ass to catch Kevin. Kevin hit the corner, went through the ally, and on the bus.

• • • • • •

Two buses and a transfer later, he was one block from the crib. He was saving for a house. He was currently living in a two bedroom apartment.

"What's up, What's up?"

"Hey baby, how are you?"

"Everything is cool, just trying to stay away from busters

and playa haters, I don't know why I came home."

"Man please." Stephanie was his lady, they'd been together six years. She was all right, he decided she was the
one he was going to keep, she was his Ghetto Queen.

"Where's my little man?"

"He's in the room sleep, don't wake him up!"

"Shit, I'm going to wake him, my boy needs to see his
daddy."

"Don't wake him up!"

"Why?" He asked with a strained look on his face.

"A woman needs to see her man . . . let him sleep." They
embraced and kissed. Kevin rubbed his hands across her
ghetto ass, spreading her cheeks apart.

"Make it clap for me baby."

Stephanie bent over and made her ass clap.
Stephanie was a former stripper, the best in town. She had
mad skills. Her pussy could smoke a cigar and blow out
the smoke. Kevin often complemented her on her many
talents.

"POW, POW, POW," her ass was clapping loud and fast.

"You like that baby?" She asked as she bent over holding
a chair.

"No doubt, you know I do." She continued to dance
making her ass cheek jerk one at a time.

"Hold on baby, let me take a shower, I've been out in

these streets all day. I need to wash this filth off me."

"Hurry up I'm horny, you gonna make me take that dick."

"Hold on, I'll be up in you in a minute."

He removed his work uniform. This consisted of tennis shoes, oversized sweats, shorts, boxers, a jacket, two shirts (different colors), and a t-shirt. He had to wear all those clothes just in case he had to put the cops on a high speed chase.

"Hurry up, take that shit off. You ain't been out their tricking have you?" Stephanie said holding his penis in her hands examining it thoroughly.

"Nah, why you tripping . . . give me my dick back." He said.

"You know I'll know when you cum. That shit better be thick!"

"Whatever, let me get in the shower."

One thing about having a chick that knew the game. If you slip, then she'll grip. Kevin used to let them rock head ho's suck him up, but he stopped after one of his partners contracted herpes. Ramon told Kevin just about every three months he gets these sores. Ramon said his shit looked like raw hamburger. Kevin swore to himself he was not going out like that.

"Stephanie count the money, it's in my pockets." Kevin stepped into the shower turning on the warm water allowing it to wash across his face. He stood there for a few minutes just to relax as he rehashed the days events.

"Damn," Stephanie yelled out. He peaked out from behind the shower curtain.

"What's wrong?"

"Damn, look at the shit stains in your draws, did you shit on yourself? Make sure you wash your ass out. That's a damn shame, a grown ass man with shit stained draws."

"You full of jokes tonight."

"Just wash that ass out," she said, they both laughed.

Kevin was a little embarrassed.

"How much money is it?" He always let her count the money. Kevin already knew how much it was though. His momma didn't raise no fool.

"Baby," she called to him.

"Yeah."

"It's $750," she said.

"That's not bad for a days work. Peel two off for yourself, put the rest up."

"How long before we have enough to buy the house baby?"

"Not long, maybe about six months or so."

"We could get it in three if you let me go back to the club."

"We've already talked about that, do you want to go

back?"

"No, I'm just saying— "

"What you saying, huh! What you saying?" He yelled loudly, turning off the water.

"Hold it down, you're going to wake the baby." Stephanie said softly holding one finger to her lips.

"Why you ask me some dumb shit like that? I told you that was a dead issue."

"I just want to help you help us baby, that's all."

"Help me! I don't need no help. The last time you worked the club scene you got raped, you musta forgot!"

"No, I didn't forget, I'll never forget a thing like that. It wasn't my fault, I didn't ask to be raped." She said beginning to cry. He walked into the bedroom.

"Look I'm sorry, I'm hurt about the situation too. I should have been there. I'm sorry, don't cry baby. Let's just drop it. I'm going to do this for us. Don't worry, I got this."

He laid down with Stephanie holding her in his arms as she cried. He could only imagine what it must be like to be violated like that. The worse part is the next day, then the next day. After the rape she had to go on with her life. He knew it was hard for her. It was hard for him. Kevin just prayed and asked for strength. Strength to help him accept all of this on a daily basis. He often asked the Lord to keep Stephanie and his little son strong

in the event he didn't come home. Kevin decided they
would start going to church. He didn't know if it would
help, it surely wouldn't hurt.

"Hey Daddy!" It was Keon his son. He walked in the
room rubbing his eyes. He was awakened by all the
commotion.

"Hey son, how's daddy's little man?" He climbed in the
bed laying his head on Kevin's chest hugging him. He fell
back to sleep. Stephanie on one side, his son on the other.

"Steph are you okay?" He asked wiping a single tear from
her face.

"Yeah, baby I'm fine."

"I'm going to put little man back in his bed." He stood up
carrying his son looking at his innocent face, suddenly his
eyes opened.

"Hey Daddy," he said. Stretching and straining his eyes.

"Hey son, I thought you were asleep."

"Daddy you wanna play a game?" He said yawning.

"It's late, what type of game do you want to play?"

"We'll play a quick game okay."

"Okay, what do you want to play?"

"Cops and robbers, I'll be the cop you be the robbers
Daddy." Kevin put him down and Keon ran to get his
badge and handcuffs.

"Let's play another game son, daddy doesn't like that

game. I tell you what little man, how about I read you a
bed time story instead."

"Okay Daddy."

"Get in the bed." Keon ran and dove in his bed.

"What story do you want me to read?"

"I want you to make up one."

"Make up one?" Kevin responded surprisingly.

"Yeah Daddy."

"Okay son. Once upon a time there was a man that had a
lot of control over many people. He could command their
lives with effortless action. Many believed that a man
with such power, a man that seemingly had everything
must be happy and without trouble. This was a man other
men would sell their souls to the devil for. But, he had a
weakness. Do you know what his weakness was?"

"No Daddy, what was his weakness?"

"His weakness son . . . his weakness was himself."

"What made him weak, Daddy?"

"That's a good question, his insecurities about himself
made him weak. He believed there was value in having
power over people, being able to control their lives and the
lives of their families. He could control others, but he
realized he had no control over himself. The lesson is a
man, a real man does not need to control others to be
called a man. A man only needs to control himself and his

emotions. Do you understand son?"

"No Daddy, I don't."

"You will when you get older son . . . you will. I love you, get some rest."

Kevin walked out of the room. Turning off the lights, he stopped and looked back at his son as he laid in bed, eyes closed, holding his teddy. He knew he needed to control himself and stop hustling.

"Stephanie, are you sleep?" He asked after returning to the dimly lit bedroom. Stephanie was lying on her stomach, her eyes appeared to be closed.

"No, baby I'm up." She said rolling over. "Come lay down with me."

Kevin laid down on top of Stephanie looking at her while caressing her delicate skin. He removed hair that was partly covering her face.

"I love you . . . you know that right?"

"Yes I know, I love you too."

Chapter Two

Kevin's days were his nights and his nights his days. When other families were up and out, he was sleep locked inside the apartment. He was a night owl, Kevin didn't get out until the sun went down. Unless of course it was the first or fifteenth, or even better, a holiday. Then he was on the streets 24/7. Kevin once hustled for 72 hours straight and cleared 5K. He had to call Stephanie to come pick up cash twice. The game can be so sweet, but it's not for everyone, it can get tricky.

It was another night in the dope hole. The sun was going down on the urban jungle. It was show time, because the freaks and crack heads came out at night. "Where them boys at?" A crack head called out. "What up?"

"What's up?" He said in reply.

"Bitch, what's up?" Kevin replied, sizing him up.

"Let me get a fifty."

"Haul ass." He said looking down the street.

"What!"

"You heard me, haul ass— DIP!"

"You don't wanna make this money?" The junkie questioned Kevin in disbelief.

"Nah, you keep your money, partner. Gone to the next man . . . DIP!"

"FUCK YOU!"

"FUCK YO MAMA . . . say something else. Get the fuck on!"

That crack head didn't want to buy anything. He just wanted Kevin to pull out his stash so he could snatch it and run. Kevin wasn't falling for the okie-doke. Besides everyone knows you can't catch a crack head. Buddy didn't want to get cut, all those fools knew he carried a razor. He had reputation for slicing people up. The crack head walked off looking at Kevin, realizing he peeped his game. He'd have to try to catch one of those other fools slipping.

It was a busy night on the avenue, a lot of foot traffic. It seemed as if all the local junkies wanted to get high. There was also a lot of people Kevin didn't know.

"Hey baby," a white chick pulled up in a S.U.V.

"What's up?"

"Come here, I need to talk to you." Kevin walked over to
the truck, mindful this could be a cop.

"What's up?" Kevin asked, walking up to the car making
every step a sure one.

"I need a hit, I need it baby."

"What you want?"

"I want it all," she said.

"No flow, no dope!" He replied sensing where this conversation was headed.

"I don't have no money."

"What you got?" As if he didn't know.

"I got this body. I'll suck you up. I'll suck your friends
up. I need a hit baby. Let me suck it, let me baby." She
said rubbing on her body showing him her breast. She
was fine. She didn't look like a crack head, but they come
in every shape, form, and fashion. If it was a little later,
Kevin would have jumped right on that. He would go into
pimp mode and make some money off her, taking her
around to all the old pops in the hood that can't get any
and let them hit her, for a small fee of course. Kevin
figured he probably could make a grand off slim. It would
only cost him $100 worth of crack. He thought to himself,
she better ride on before he turned her out.

"Nah, baby girl I'm straight, next time." She drove off, moving on to the next man. Kevin just sat back and watched this shit unfold. He knew she was running the same game on him. Kevin was curious to see how he was going to react. It took about five minutes for everything to go down. He knew it, buddy got in the truck. Kevin hoped he knew what he was doing. Kevin wasn't going any where, he was on a mission to make that money.

"Yo, What up?"

"What up?"

"Let me get that dime up out ya."

"I ain't got no dimes . . . twenties or better."

"All I got is a ten."

"That ain't enough."

He walked off from the woman, looking down the block he saw one of his best customers, the principal at one of the local high schools. Kevin greeted him with excitement and respect.

"What's up Playa?" He asked bending down to the half rolled up window.

"What's up?" The principal said.

"Let me get five up out ya." This man gets high, that's five cookies. The scary shit was he would be back. Kevin believed he was tricking with those young high school girls. He'd be on the ten o'clock news sooner or later, the brother was starting to look bad. He couldn't possibly hold it together much longer. "All right playa, I'll see ya," Kevin told him as he drove off rolling up his dark tinted windows.

It was going to be a good night. Eight o'clock, it was still early. Kevin had made about $500, it was break time. He walked across the street to the Chinese store to get a sandwich.

"Papa-San what's up!" He liked joking with the Chinese people. It was all good, they are out here hustling too. They were just in different games, but it was the same field.

"Papa-San don't act like you don't hear me."

"What do you want? Buy something or leave the store."

"Calm down you chop stick using, rice eating, ghetto hustler." He said pointing at him and laughing.

"Up yours, Ready. Buy something or get out." Everyone on the streets knew Kevin as Ready. Kevin picked up the name because he was always ready for whatever.

"All right calm down!" Ready leaned over to look at the sandwiches in the glass cooler. "Yeah, let me get that ham and cheese sub."

"This one?" Papa-San asked, touching the sandwich.

"Nah, the big one man, the big one. Don't try and give me that little shit."

"That's it?"

"Yeah, let me get this water too." Ready said reaching down in a bucket of ice removing a liter of water.

"$5.50," said Papa-San.

"$5.50, you trying to rob a brother." He gave the attendant his money. "Keep the change," he said walking out of the store.

He loved joking with them. He didn't mess around too much, they would bust a cap in your ass. They got AK's, AR's, 45's, an arsenal. When you walk in you might only see two men, but it's ten people in there, all strapped to the teeth. He would mess with them, but he didn't fuck with them, if you know the meaning.

"Ready," a voice called from down the street. He waited for the body to come out of darkness.

"Who dat?" Ready yelled back.

"It's your boy Smitty." Dean Smith, an ex C.E.O. of a major telecommunications company turned crack head. This brother smoked up his job, house, cars, marriage, the kids college fund, the dog, everything. He still thought he was a C.E.O. Smith had on the same suit for two years.

"What they do Smitty?"

"Ready, my brother, how are things?"

"Yeah, yeah what?"

"Listen, I need your help, I'm having a slight cash flow

problem. I was wondering if you would be so kind as to
spot me $100 until next week?"

"I don't have $100 Smitty."

"Oh! I'm sorry to hear that. I guess times are tough all
over. Well if you don't have the money, I'll take some
crack." He said, extending his hand.

"You funny Smitty, funny as hell. I can't help you
brother, spread your hustle."

"Thank you for your time Mr. Ready, I'll be speaking with
you soon." Smith buttoned his weather beaten overcoat
and walked down the block.

     Ready knew this crack was a beast. He never tried
it, but he had witnessed the effects of this monster first
hand. Women and men prostituting themselves for it.
Some go as far as to sell the bodies of their children. Life
was crazy. He walked back to his spot and posted up
ready to make his money. A chocolate Impala rolled up.

"What's up baby?" It was Monica, one of his old chicken
heads.

"What up Slim?"

"I've missed you, you don't return my beeps when I call."

"Well you know I'm on my job, making this money."

"You can still give a sister a call, I just wanted to give you
some that's all."

"That's all, huh?"

"Yeah, that used to be enough."

Ready bent over leaning in the car looking at her fat coochie bulging trough her shorts. That thang was so fat it looked like a pile of dirty clothes. Most women have a V print, when he looked down at Monica she had a W. That monkey was fat.

"What's up, what you doing right now?" He asked rubbing on her.

"Get in," she said as she grabbed his hand pushing it hard against her. He paused for a moment while looking at Monica and rubbing her, she was creaming, he could feel the moisture from her.

"Get in," She said again in a soft yearning voice. He walked around the car, opened the door and sat down.

"Where to?" Monica asked.

"Pull around behind the store." Ready pointed the way.

"Behind the store! What happened to the hotel?"

"I don't have time for that." He looked at her with a raised brow. "What's up you want this or what?"

"You got a rubber?" She asked.

"Yeah."

Ready took the rubber out of his jacket opening it as she pulled down his sweats. He put the condom on the dash board, as he assisted her in removing his layers of clothes.

"Give it to me." She said, asking for the condom. Monica
put the condom in her mouth, grabbing his penis, jacking
it softly. She bent down putting him in her mouth.
"Suck it baby, suck it." She was sucking it good. He
could feel her slob running down his balls.
"HUM, HUM, HUM" She was humming making her jaws
vibrate. She raised up wiping the slob from her mouth.
Ready looked down and the rubber was on.
"You ready for this now?"
"Yeah, take your shorts off." Monica leaned back in the
seat raising her hips to wiggle out of her skin tight shorts.
She had the fattest, hairiest cat on the planet. He stuck his
self right in it, up and down, in and out.
"You like it?"
"I love it." She said moaning out the words. He had her
squealing like a pig. He enjoyed watching himself go in
and out of her.
"I'm bout to bust." He started going faster and harder.
Ready came hard, he could feel the fluid leaving his body
in rapid gushes. It felt like a water balloon bursting on
concrete. That's a perfect way to describe it, because they
had a problem.
"Oh shit!" He said in disgust.
"What happened? What's wrong?" Monica asked in a
huff.

"The condom broke."

"Broke, the condom broke . . . Ready I know you didn't shoot off in me. Tell me you didn't nut in me."

"I came in you. It's in you. The rubber broke. What was I supposed to do?" He asked, looking at her.

"Take it out, take it out." She said, grabbing him to make sure the rubber was broke.

"Fuck that, all I know is I hope you're not burning." He said as he removed the remaining part of the condom from the base of his penis.

"Burning, Ready I know you just didn't try me like some ho!"

"You are a ho. You just got fucked in your car, behind the store, in the dope hole. You're a ho."

"Fuck you Ready!"

"You just did . . . don't be mad at me cause the rubber broke. You need to shave that hairy ass pussy you got." He told her pulling up his clothes.

"If I'm pregnant I'm going to keep the baby."

"Bitch . . . are you crazy?"

"Yeah, I'll be your bitch!" She said wiping his juice from her body.

"We'll see, let me out this motherfucker. Oh yeah, by the way, thanks for the head." Ready sarcastically muttered while exiting the car. He walked back over to the spot, he thought he probably missed about two hundred dollars.

"Ready."

"What up?"

"Let me get a twenty." He made the exchange and moved on, he was angry because he'd wasted a lot of time.

"Ready," it was the freak he just screwed.

"What!" He yelled, throwing his hands out.

"I'll see yo punk ass in nine months!"

"WHATEVER BITCH!" He yelled, while Monica sped off down the street.

Ready knew he had made a mistake, *Dumb Ass Me* he thought. He had enough of these streets tonight, it was time to take it to the house.

OH, SO YOU THOUGHT
THE INTRIGUING TALE OF MAYHEM
AND DECEIT WAS OVER?

LET'S TALK ABOUT IT . . . . . .

E-MAIL ME AT
WWW.MICHAELGAINER.NET
WITH YOUR COMMENTS ABOUT THE
QUESTIONS ON THE FOLLOWING
PAGE . . . . . .

QUESTIONS TO PONDER . . . . . .

WHY DO YOU THINK JUSTIN
CHEATED?

DID THE "ROOSTER" HAVE A HAND IN
JUSTIN'S ADULT LIFE?

WHAT WOULD YOU HAVE DONE IF
YOU WERE IN JUSTIN'S PREDICAMENT?

INTRODUCING EDEN. WHAT IS THIS
WOMAN REALLY ABOUT?

IS ALEXIS A LUCKY WOMAN OR WHAT?
JUSTIN IS FINE, SMART, AND HAS BIG
POCKETS!

THANKS FOR SHARING YOUR
THOUGHTS!

IS A MAN BORN WITH HIS
CHARACTER? OR IS CHARACTER
ATTAINED THROUGH HIS
EXPERIENCES?

<u>YOU</u> <u>DECIDE</u>.
READ MICHAEL GAINER'S
THRILLING PREQUEL TO
DUMB AS ME:

<u>JUSTIN</u>

Exit From Paradise

AVAILABLE SOON FROM
PLUTONIUM PUBLISHING,LLC

VISIT US ONLINE @ WWW.MICHAELGAINER.NET

AT THE OFFICIAL MICHAEL GAINER WEBSITE YOU'LL FIND:

- ☐ Chapter Excerpts from Current and Upcoming Releases

- ☐ Self Publishing Tips

- ☐ Sign Guest Book

- ☐ Michael Gainer's Official E-mail

- ☐ Plus Much More!

www.michaelgainer.net

I'd love to hear from you!
Questions? Comments? Or just
want to check in to see what's up.
Drop me a line at my state of the art
Guest Book at
www.michaelgainer.net.

Michael